COPYRIGHTED MATERIAL

Copyright © 2019 by Olivia Ash.
Cover and art copyright © 2019 by Amalia Chitulescu
Book design and layout copyright © 2019 by Olivia Ash.

This novel is a work of fiction. Names, characters, places and incidents are either products of the author's imagination or used fictitiously. Any resemblance to actual events, locales, or persons, living, dead, or undead, is entirely coincidental.

All rights reserved.

No part of this publication can be reproduced or transmitted in any form or by any means, electronic or mechanical, without permission in writing from S. M. Boyce, L. L. C.

www.wispvine.com

1st Edition

BOOKS BY OLIVIA ASH

The Nighthelm Guardian Series

City of the Sleeping Gods

City of Fractured Souls

City of the Enchanted Queen

Demon Queen Saga

Princes of the Underworld

Wars of the Underworld

Mistress of the Underworld

Sentinel Saga

By Dahlia Leigh and Olivia Ash

The Shadow Shifter

The Demon Prince

The Rogue Alchemist

STAY CONNECTED

Olivia Ash occasionally takes over the Wispvine Publishing social media channels on Facebook, Instagram, and Twitter.

Olivia also likes to hang out with Lila Jean in their Facebook group specifically for readers like you to come together and share their lives and interests, especially regarding the hot guys from their reverse harem novels. Please check it out and join in whenever you get the chance! Everyone in there is amazing, and you'll fit right in.

https://www.facebook.com/groups/LilaJeanOliviaAsh/

Sign up for email alerts of new releases AND exclusive access to bonus content, book recommendations, and more!

https://wispvine.com/newsletter/nighthelm-academy-email-signup/

Enjoying the series? Awesome! Help others discover The Nighthelm Guardian Series by leaving a review at Amazon.

http://mybook.to/Nighthelm1

CITY OF FRACTURED SOULS

BOOK TWO OF THE NIGHTHELM GUARDIAN SERIES

OLIVIA ASH

BOOK DESCRIPTION

If you're banished to the shadowy realm within Ripthorn Mountain, you die.

The mountain's fractured magic seeps into the bones of humans, slowly draining the life from their bodies with every step they take. It has been a death sentence for as long as anyone in the kingdom of Nighthelm can remember.

And now, it's Sophia's fate.

Banished to the depths of the savage mountain, Sophia and her men are left with a choice: find their way to the surface, or die.

But there are hungry beasts in the mountain.

An ancient evil hunts Andreas, determined to end an old feud the wraith shifter had nothing to do with. And as it stalks them, ever closer, the clock is ticking for Zeke and Edric. Even with all their strength and magic, their human bodies can't survive the mountain much longer.

But in the darkness, there's a glimmer of light.

In the depths of the mountain, in the farthest shadow of the darkest cavern, a young woman lies suspended in glowing crystal. Wounded and bloody, the girl stokes the depths of Sophia's memory, reminding her of another time, of a life when she wasn't broken. Close to death and unable to move, it's clear the girl has the answers Sophia needs.

And now, Sophia has a new choice to make—between her mission, or her men.

Her men are slowly dying. Monsters stalk her every step. But Sophia is a survivor, and she won't let the mountain win.

City of the Fractured Souls is a full-length reverse harem novel. Get ready for a breathtaking story, soulmate romance, lip-biting love scenes, mind-blowing magic, one kickass heroine, three gorgeous men, lots of toned muscles, fights to the death, and edge-of-your-seat action.

CONTENTS

Chapter One	1
Chapter Two	17
Chapter Three	25
Chapter Four	37
Chapter Five	47
Chapter Six	59
Chapter Seven	69
Chapter Eight	79
Chapter Nine	89
Chapter Ten	101
Chapter Eleven	111
Chapter Twelve	121
Chapter Thirteen	127
Chapter Fourteen	133
Chapter Fifteen	145
Chapter Sixteen	149
Chapter Seventeen	155
Chapter Eighteen	161
Chapter Nineteen	165
Chapter Twenty	173
Chapter Twenty-One	177
Chapter Twenty-Two	185
Chapter Twenty-Three	193
Chapter Twenty-Four	201
Chapter Twenty-Five	207
Chapter Twenty-Six	213
Chapter Twenty-Seven	221
Chapter Twenty-Eight	229
Chapter Twenty-Nine	233
Chapter Thirty	239

Chapter Thirty-One	245
Chapter Thirty-Two	253
Chapter Thirty-Three	259
Chapter Thirty-Four	263
Chapter Thirty-Five	269
Chapter Thirty-Six	275
Chapter Thirty-Seven	279
Chapter Thirty-Eight	285
Chapter Thirty-Nine	291
Chapter Forty	297
You're Missing Out...	301
About the Author	303

CHAPTER ONE

SOPHIA

Sneaking through the dark streets in the Shade, Sophia followed Andreas, Edric, and Ezekiel. They stuck to the shadows, hoping to avoid detection from the guard that had increased their patrols in the past week. Winston had yet to blame them for the death of Headmistress Mittle, but with the rise in the number of guards, everyone in the group knew it was only a matter of time before they would come knocking down the door of Ezekiel's estate.

Andreas had mentioned some of the abandoned buildings outside of the Shade that were left empty since the wraiths moved in. People of Nighthelm were still wary of the race, even after the king had given them citizenship, and they avoided the Shade at all costs.

That worked for them.

"Just there," Andreas said, pointing to an old tavern and inn. "What do you think, Zeke?"

Zeke narrowed his eyes on the old building in disrepair. He nodded. "Yup. It'll do."

"Good," Edric said. "Let's get set up."

Haris groaned. Sophia patted his side. The poor guy would be cramped, but it was a temporary fix. With all the hope she had within her, she knew they would find the heirs and get this whole mess cleared.

"We'll have to go back and ensure the wards and traps are set at my place," Ezekiel said. "And gather some supplies needed to keep the ones here going. It will take a lot of power to keep them active. Someone will take notice, but hopefully not before we can locate the heirs."

Sophia nodded. "How long do you think we will have?"

Ezekiel shrugged. "One week. Two tops. But I can work on devising a way to keep the minimum power needed to make this work for as long as necessary."

"Good," Sophia said. "That should buy us enough time." At least she hoped.

"Let's get set up then," Andreas said and continued forward. "The beds will probably smell, but I can see about getting some new linens from the Shade."

"We'll make do," Sophia said.

Once inside, the smell of dust and rot filled their

noses. Haris groaned his displeasure. The main room was cramped, and only simple stools were available for sitting. In the dining room portion of the building, there were a few booths in dire need of oil and a good polish, but they at least had solid tables.

"I'll get started on the wards and traps here," Ezekiel said and got to work.

"I'll look for anything of use," Andreas said.

Edric stood in the shadows in the corner of the room. "I'll keep watch. Go find your room."

Sophia nodded and motioned for Haris to stay put. He grunted but obeyed. With a pat on his snout, she turned and climbed up the stairs to locate her room. There were ten of them to choose from. She wanted one that overlooked the streets outside. If the guards were to ever find them, she wanted to make sure that she could see them before they could see her.

She took the first room she came to and dropped her bags on the bed. Must and mildew filled the air. Nothing opening the shutters couldn't take care of. The small fireplace at the far wall would provide light and warmth during the chilly nights.

There wasn't enough room for Haris. He would have to sleep on the main floor. He wouldn't be happy about it, but it wasn't safe anywhere else for him, and Sophia couldn't stand the thought of being too far from him either.

With a sigh, she returned to the main floor to

break the news to her yakshi friend. She could already imagine his reaction.

As she approached the final step on the staircase, Andreas shouted in glee. Sophia instantly went to find out what it was about.

Andreas stood behind the old bar, pulling out jugs of what she presumed was ale. The smile on his face was wide and there was a glint in his eyes. She shook her head and took a seat on the other side of the bar.

Edric joined them. "What's all this racket about?"

"I found ale!" Andreas said, dragging out "ale" in a singsong voice. He found a few tin cups and rinsed them out with his skin full of water. "Come on, Zeke!"

"I'll join you once I'm finished," he said, voice sounding strained.

Sophia wondered if it took too much out of him to cast the wards and shield the place. In a previous discussion, they had talked about how the illusion would be that the building would appear uninhabited from the outside. It all seemed so intricate, but she never thought to ask if it drained him physically.

Meanwhile, Andreas passed along the cups between the three of them. He held his in the air and said, "Not a bad way to end the night, if I do say so myself."

Ezekiel nodded and took a sip of his ale. "Indeed."

Haris let out another long grumble. Sophia knew it was his way of voicing his displeasure with being cooped up inside the small inn. Poor thing. Sophia sympathized with him. She went to him and patted her friend's muscular, green flank, assuring him that everything was okay. Though being stuck inside plaster and stone walls wasn't ideal, it was the situation they had to deal with.

Ezekiel approached Sophia, careful of Haris's antlers as he had just shaken them again. If they weren't careful, they would probably get a good-sized hole in an arm or their side, getting too close to the creature when he shook himself. "He's not thrilled, is he?" Zeke asked.

Sophia shook her head and continued to do her best to comfort her friend. "No. He's used to the freedom of the woods."

Haris snorted and stomped his hoof in agreement.

"Did the wards and traps go well?" she asked.

He nodded. "They'll do for the night. I'll strengthen and expand them tomorrow. But we are safely hidden for now."

Though the inn was near the small side of things, Haris made that size smaller. He was large enough that his antlers scraped along the ceiling if he stood at his full height. As it was, he had to keep himself hunched over, head held lower than normal. He groaned again and lay on an old tattered rug near the fireplace along the far wall, trying his best to not bump into anything and growing more agitated at the cramped space he wasn't accustomed to.

"Are you sure he'll be all right here?" Ezekiel asked. The expression in his features let Sophia know he truly felt sorry for Haris, and that made her love him all the more.

She smiled and gave a short nod. "He will be. He's just not used to being inside confining structures."

"I was sure Howard would crap himself when we first opened the front door and smuggled Haris inside." Ezekiel chuckled.

Sophia joined him in the short laugh as she recalled the moment as well. That was the second night they were at his estate, just before the increase in patrols could no longer be ignored. The sorcerer always made her feel lighter and contented, and she loved that he'd opened his home without question to her and to Edric and Andreas. Especially the last two, considering they had been something close to enemies growing up. Well, they wouldn't mix company willingly, that was for sure. But all that had changed when Sophia came into the picture. She joined the men in a brotherhood stronger than she ever could imagine.

"I'll get that fire going," Ezekiel said as he slapped his hands together. Sparks formed in his palms, shinning bright blue and purple. He pointed to the fireplace, and sparks shot out from his fingertips and caught the wood. A warm orange glow and warmth filled the room. "Better?" he asked Haris.

Haris huffed and rested his head on his front legs. Ezekiel shrugged and rejoined Sophia's side.

Edric approached them, handing both her and Ezekiel a cup of ale. "Haris will be fine." He glanced at the large, green beast. "Won't you boy?"

Haris huffed in response and turned his head away, which made Sophia giggle. Her yakshi friend still wasn't quite sure of Edric or Ezekiel. Andreas, her wraith shifter and protector, Haris liked, probably because of his dual nature, but the other two of her men he still worked on warming up to.

She supposed they were *all* still getting used to each other. She looked at each of her men just hanging out and making the best of a sour situation and smiled. A month ago, the three of them would've been at each other's throats, as they had been for the past twenty years, growing up in competition with each other atNighthelm Academy. Seeing them with her, united for her cause and so faithfully, filled her heart with joy.

She took a sip of her ale and sat in one of the booths next to Andreas. As she relished in the spices and warmth the drink gave, Andreas tapped his cup against hers and downed his ale in two big gulps.

As she finished the last of her drink, she sank back against the booth, letting her body relax. Well, as much as they could considering their circumstances. The heat from the fire washed over her and she sighed. Being with her protectors—her lovers—had filled Sophia with a happiness that had eluded her for the past eighteen years. She felt strong, capable, and more in tune with her magic than she'd ever been.

She flexed her hands, sensing her magic just below the surface, simmering, ready to be utilized at her command. But this time, it wasn't perilous. Those around her weren't in danger of her magic bursting out of her like a raging inferno, incinerating everything within a fifty-foot radius. Despite all his flaws, maybe Grindel had actually taught her to control it with discipline. Perhaps, all those years he pushed her through training had been worth it.

Her heart panged when she thought of him. His loss still stung anew with each thought of him that crossed her mind. Tears burned and nipped at her eyes.

Andreas shifted, drawing her attention as he took her hand. He squeezed, providing support and strength. He definitely seemed more in tune with her emotions than Edric and Ezekiel.

Edric circled the room, refilling their cups. Once finished, he lifted his cup into the air and said, "A toast."

"What are we toasting?" Ezekiel asked, lifting his

cup into the air, a huge, cheesy smile stretching his lips.

"Our victory." Edric's intense gaze met Sophia's, and she melted a little. The heat of desire and love in them was relentless. "And to Sophia. For bringing all of us together."

She lifted her cup, and Andreas did as well.

"Here, here!" they said in unison then tipped their cups to their mouths, taking in long pulls of the ale.

Ezekiel wiped his mouth with the back of his hand. "You might rethink that last part after we've lived together for another few weeks."

Edric chuckled. "Fair point."

Shouts from outside drew Sophia's attention. She stood from the booth and went to the window to look outside. Guards stood in formed ranks on the streets in front of the Shade, their superiors shouting orders, and all of them armed with swords and appearing ready to fight. They were likely looking for Andreas, which they probably hoped would lead to the rest of them.

Ezekiel came up behind her and set his hands on her shoulders. She leaned into him with a sigh.

"We're safe, I promise," he said. "They can't see us. The cloaking spells will only allow them to see the building as an empty structure. No lights shine through the windows. It's as if we were never here. No one in Nighthelm can break the enchantments."

But Sophia knew Winston Kent had friends in high places, and sorcerers from other kingdoms were probably already summoned to Nighthelm to help him break Ezekiel's powerful enchantments. Especially since the two parted on not-so-great terms. Winston wanted her, and Sophia wanted nothing to do with him. With Winston's wounded pride, it was only a matter of time before someone who could break the enchantments showed.

Haris snorted behind them. She turned to her friend as he shifted nervously on the spot he'd claimed as his sleeping nest. He looked out of place in the small, cramped space, but it wasn't safe for him—for any of them—out in the Witch Woods anymore. The city was dangerous for them as well. The entire city guard hunted them. And with the grimms that had threatened her life and attacked their group on several occasions within the woods, they had nowhere else to go.

Sophia sighed.

Refocus.

Branded as fugitives, staying in Ezekiel's ancestral home was not an option. At some point, they'd have to leave this dusty old inn as well.

Winston and the Nameless Master were after them. In order to survive and get through what they were bound to face sooner than later, they needed a plan for finding the heirs.

She turned from the window. "As much as I would love to loiter here and pretend like we are living normal lives, I still have a job to do."

"Find the heirs to the throne," Edric said, setting his cup on the table near the couch.

She nodded. "The oracles have tasked me to do this, and I won't let them down." She flexed her fingers and rolled her shoulders, eager to get back into action. "Besides, I'm sure when we find them, they will pardon us for our crimes. Then, Winston and the duchess won't be able to touch us. They won't have the power in Nighthelm to so much as even point a finger at us."

"Let's think... where else could we look to find information on the heirs?" Edric asked.

"Let's figure out where we have been," Andreas said. "Then we can explore where is left to look."

Sophia smiled as she let out a breath she hadn't realized she was holding. Her men were with her regardless. Even so much as taking on a task that was appointed to her.

"We need to do some research in the castle archives about the royal family," Edric suggested. "That would be the first place I would look. It's supposed to hold all the information regarding them."

"The last time I tried to get into the castle, the stone and brick rearranged itself and wouldn't let me in." Before that night, Sophia had no idea an inanimate stone structure could do that. But magic was powerful. She'd seen it do mystical things, especially at the command of someone capable and dynamic. Ezekiel had impressed her several times with the things he could do. She even surprised herself with how much control she had gained over her own powers.

"The ruler controls the castle," Ezekiel said as he paced the room. "Perhaps the duchess had been made aware of your gifts by the headmistress and wanted to keep you out."

"If that's the case, then we can't go anywhere near the castle or it will probably trap us inside, like rabbits in a snare," Sophia said.

"Where else is there to look?" Andreas asked. "There has to be information somewhere."

Ezekiel snapped his fingers and said, "What about this? We'll go to the Metropolis Library and infiltrate the forbidden section. But we'll have to be very careful."

Andreas snorted from the sofa. "Oh yeah, nothing more dangerous than sneaking into a library."

"Coming from someone who probably has never read a book." Ezekiel made a face at Andreas.

Andreas looked appalled. "Hey, I've read a book."

"When?" Ezekiel asked.

Andreas shrugged. "In the academy."

"That was like, fifteen years ago, during our

primary education." Ezekiel shook his head, his lips twisted up into a wry grin.

"Yeah, but I *have* read a book. We can't all engage in carnal relations with tomes on conjuring and spell-casting like you, Zeke." Andreas snorted.

Edric crossed his arms and gave the other men a hard look. "Can we focus on the task at hand, please?"

Andreas shrugged and gestured to Edric to continue, as he leaned into the corner of the booth, draping his arm over the top.

"Do you know the workings of the library?" Edric asked Ezekiel.

"Yes." He stood a bit taller. "I know every entrance and exit on every floor."

"Good. Then you'll lead us in," Edric said.

Another loud shout and a bang filled the room, and Sophia looked out the window again.

"Are you sure they can't get in?" she asked Ezekiel.

"If they try, they get a nice little zap. They don't know we're here, and they can't come inside. If they manage to get through the initial wards, albeit painfully, alarms would sound here. I've laid traps throughout the house and on the grounds leading to the house. If the alarm sounds, we will have the time and chance to escape."

She nodded. She trusted him and his abilities to ward and trap and provide them a means for at least temporary shelter. But the city would likely turn against them for killing the beloved Headmistress Mittle of the Nighthelm Academy. Though Winston hadn't publicly announced the death of the headmistress, it was inevitable he would soon. Then every citizen of Nighthelm—every guard, every merchant, every noble person—would know what they had done and would hate them for it. But they didn't truly understand what was going on inside the walls of their own city. Blind faith and all.

"Perfect," she said. Haris groaned.

She approached him and pet his flank. "It's okay, my friend. This won't last forever."

He nodded his head and snorted.

Edric moved to stand behind Sophia. She melted into him, breathing him in. In his arms, she felt safe. Protected. But she wasn't sure she could return the gesture for him or the others. He was isolated, as were Andreas and Ezekiel, from their jobs and families. She knew that Edric's post as commander of the city guard was part of who he was. And he pushed that aside... for her.

She vowed she would make it right for him and Andreas and Ezekiel. They had sacrificed everything for her, and she would be damned if she didn't do the same thing. For twelve years she didn't have a real family. Now she had one. The men were her team. And she loved them dearly and would go to the ends of the world and back for them. Considering what they were up against—the duchess, the city guards, and the sorcerers of Nighthelm Castle, grimms, and a Nameless Master with more power than she'd ever thought possible to exist within one person—she just might have to.

CHAPTER TWO

SOPHIA

During the dead of night, when the streets were clear of most guards, they snuck out of the inn and traveled across the city to the Metropolis, a museum and library. They kept to the shadows to prevent being seen, and Ezekiel cast a cloaking spell for when they were on the more heavily guarded roads.

When they reached the Metropolis—a large three-story, white and black stone building, circular in shape—Ezekiel used a special, enchanted key to open one of the side doors which was covered by vines growing up one side of the smooth structure. Sophia remembered breaking into the building through one of the windows on the second floor, which she had reached from the domed roof. She was tempted to tell Ezekiel about that, but she suspected he'd already known about her secret activities as he nearly caught her that particular night.

"No one uses this entrance, so there shouldn't be any guards nearby," he said, as he pushed the door open for them to enter.

"I'll still keep a look out, just in case," Edric said.

Ezekiel nodded.

One by one, they filed into an empty foyer that led to the cavernous, opulent lobby. Ezekiel led them across the marble-floored room to the far side, where they came up against another locked door. He opened that and led them down another corridor to yet another door.

"How many secret doors are in this place?" Andreas asked.

"As many as there needs to be," Ezekiel answered, his voice was flat yet patient.

Andreas frowned. "Is that some kind of clever sorcerer riddle?"

"Both of you shut it," Edric said, "and concentrate on what we need to do."

Ezekiel opened the next door that led to a dark staircase going down into the basement. There were no torches available, so both Ezekiel and Sophia created balls of green light to light their way. Ezekiel grinned at her over the glowing sphere in his hand. She did the same.

Sophia loved using magic with Ezekiel. She didn't

have to hide her abilities any longer. In the future, she hoped they would have time for him to teach her some simple spells that would be useful for defense. For now, she would just have to rely on him to use his magic to defend them in the event something happened.

The air changed when they made it down more than two levels and reached the bottom of the stone stairs, as though they descended into damnation itself. The damp air chilled Sophia, and a shiver rushed down her spine. Something besides the cool, stale air bothered her. She couldn't put her finger on the source, but it seemed like they stepped into a different realm altogether. She knew they were underneath the library. The stone walls were rough and jagged. The ceiling was low and jagged as well. The state of the corridor made Sophia wonder if the builders had given up on this part of the building, but there was something else that gave off that different feel down here. And judging by the looks on the others' faces, she wasn't the only one experiencing the odd sensation.

Andreas shifted his gaze, his hand going to the dagger strapped to one leg. "Anyone else feel that?"

Edric nodded. "Be ready for anything."

As they moved down the dark corridor, Ezekiel in the lead, Sophia behind him, and Edric and Andreas taking up the rear, glimmers of light shone in the distant darkness. Light that seemed to bounce up and down, like they bobbed in water.

Sophia's pulse spiked as adrenaline shot through her bloodstream. Every muscle in her body tensed in preparation. After being cooped up for days inside the old inn, she ached for some action. After all, being raised in the Witch Woods, training every day with a sword and bow and arrow and her bare hands, she lived for the thrill of the hunt. And that's what this felt like.

A *hunt*.

A few more feet, and Sophia knew what waited for them in the darkness. "Wisps," she murmured. Others called them fool's fire.

They were fairy-like creatures, no bigger than fruit gnats, which were known to lure men to their deaths out in the marshes of the Witch Woods. But in here, their presence didn't make sense. They were one of the many dangerous beings that lurked in the forest. What were they doing inside the basement of a library in the middle of Nighthelm?

Sophia touched Ezekiel's arm to get him to stop. They needed to confer with each other and find a way around those creatures, because they were obviously on the right path. Someone was protecting whatever was behind the wall of wisps.

"Those are wisps," Sophia said, referencing the inviting lights bouncing around in the air thirty feet from where they stood huddled together. "They are very rare creatures, hard to capture. Whoever put them there doesn't want anyone to pass."

"I heard wisps will appear when there is something valuable nearby," Andreas added.

Sophia nodded. "Yes, there is lore to support that theory."

"There have been rumors for years about a secret vault in the basement," Ezekiel said. "A vault that contains long-buried secrets about the origins of Nighthelm and the royal family."

"That is definitely what we're looking for," Sophia said.

Edric's eyes narrowed as he looked at the wisps. "How do we combat them?"

Sophia had handled wisps before, during one of her many patrols through the woods. They had tried to lure her toward a pit of venomous vipers, with their warm, inviting light and melodic, chiming voices, but she'd managed to resist by blindfolding herself and moving pass them carefully. The trick was not to look into their light. Only within their light did the wisps have power.

"Their power resides in their light," she said. "The only way through them is without seeing."

"You want us to close our eyes and walk through them?" Andreas asked.

She shook her head. "Has to be a blindfold, or you risk accidentally looking."

"Let me try a dark smoke spell first," Ezekiel said. "Maybe it will darken them enough for us to pass by."

Edric nodded. "Do it."

After handing over the ball of green light to Edric, who clutched the sphere warily, Ezekiel moved out of their huddle and walked toward the wisps. When he was about fifteen feet away, he stopped and clapped his hands together. He rubbed them vigorously against one another, and Sophia could see the blue sparks of his magic undulating over his fingers. His head was lowered, and she wondered if he'd closed his eyes so he couldn't be influenced by the wisps. She heard a few mumbled words from him, but nothing she could discern. Within a few moments, a black sphere formed between his palms, and as he drew his hands out, the dark mass swelled in size.

Once the swirling, black smoke nearly filled the corridor from side to side, Ezekiel pushed the magic toward the wisps. He returned to stand with the group and watched.

"Kind of looks like you, Andreas," Ezekiel joked.

Andreas punched the sorcerer in the shoulder, hard enough to send him stumbling sideways. "You're a funny guy, Zeke."

Sophia shook her head and smiled. Watching her men rib each other filled her with joy. A month ago, she suspected that Andreas would've shifted into his wraith form and terrorized Ezekiel for his remark. But not anymore. Now, it was like two brothers picking on each other.

The dark smoke flowed down the corridor and enveloped the wisps, snuffing out the light, plunging them back into darkness with only the green balls of witchlight illuminating the immediate area around them.

"That should keep the wisps at bay until we pass by," Ezekiel said.

They regrouped and moved down the corridor. Soon, they stepped through the dark smoke, and the balls of witchlight diminished with each step until they disappeared altogether. Sophia could no longer see Ezekiel in front of her. With caution, she extended her left hand behind her, locking fingers with Edric.

She didn't want to get separated from her men in the darkness. They would have a better chance of completing the mission together. Her right hand went to the hilt of her sword, though she was wary of the possibility of having to draw it in a tight space. What if she accidentally harmed one of her men?

"Be on guard." Edric must've picked up on her thoughts. Knowing him, Sophia figured he had his hand on the hilt of his own sword as well.

She took another two steps and was blinded by a sudden flash of bright, white light. Gasping, she clamped her eyes shut, but she was too late. The damage had been done. All she could see behind her lids were dancing spots of light.

"Sophia!" Edric called for her.

"I'm here," she said, as she reached out with her hands.

He grabbed her hands and pulled her to him. "Where are the others?"

"I don't know." She risked opening one eye, but quickly closed it again when the light pierced her retina and pain stabbed her head. She called out, "Andreas? Ezekiel?"

The only answer was the miniscule tinkling sound of wisp laughter.

CHAPTER THREE

EZEKIEL

*E*zekiel stopped mid-step, frowning at the dancing light in front of him. Something was wrong. Confused, he looked around. He glanced down at his hands, wiggling his fingers. He was sure he'd produced some kind of magic only moments ago.

He shook his head, trying to clear it of the fog that seemed to cloud his mind, and moved forward, following the warm light that seemed to lead him to something extraordinary. *That,* he was certain of. Maybe it would be buried treasure. He had read about pirates from the Serpent Sea burying the gold and jewels they had stolen from vessels on small, uninhabited islands.

Wouldn't that be something to find?

Delighted by the prospects, he picked up his pace, hurrying after the moving light. He took another few steps, a shuffling noise echoing behind him. He quickly glanced over his shoulder. Startled, he stopped and turned around to face Andreas.

"What are you doing here?" he asked.

Andreas frowned, and a puzzled expression took over. "I don't know. Following you, I think." The wraith-shifter blinked at him.

Now that Ezekiel wasn't looking directly into the light, he too became confused. Or, maybe, less confused? He surveyed the corridor they stood in. It was different than before. "Are we in the right place?"

Andreas looked at the jagged ceiling and walls, then back to Ezekiel. "I'm not sure." His frown deepened. He rubbed his face with both hands. "I don't feel right. My head is clouded."

Ezekiel shook his head again, removing some more of the fog. He remembered Andreas from before. He also remembered Edric… and Sophia.

Yes, Sophia. Beautiful Sophia.

They were all here, together. Weren't they? He peered over Andreas's shoulder into the darkness behind them. "Where are Edric and Sophia?"

They came here to do something. Something important. He just couldn't remember exactly what that something was. He couldn't quite recall where here even was. Ezekiel pressed his fingers to the wall on his right and closed his eyes. He focused his thoughts and tried to think through the remaining fog that clouded his mind. He picked up sensations from the rock—a tingling feeling, power, familiarity. All of the books on spells and casting and conjuring called to him from beyond the stone wall. He remembered.

The library.

They were in the dark passageways below the Metropolis searching for… he couldn't quite grasp the memory that tapped at the back of his mind.

Ezekiel! Andreas! A female voice whispered from somewhere far, far away. The words drifted on the wind, yet no breeze so much as tickled the scruff on his cheeks. Everything around him was thick and oppressive, and the damp air pressed down on him with the scent of mold and age.

"I think…" He trailed off as confusion set in again. "I think we're lost, Andreas."

Andreas shook his head as if he tried to clear fog from his mind as well. He glanced behind him at the thick darkness that closed in on them more and more as the seconds trickled on. He turned back around and pointed down the corridor. "Let's keep following the light."

Ezekiel looked into the shimmering blue and white glow. His doubts and concerns faded. Following the light made sense. Going into the deepest of the dark didn't. Danger lurked in darkness. Everyone knew that. Besides, the light seemed so warm and inviting. Nodding, he said, "That's a good idea."

"Ezekiel!" A female voice called to him again.

The sound made his heart skip a beat. He knew the lilt of that voice. Every syllable she spoke was a melody in his head. He longed for that voice. An ache built in his gut and he frowned, stopping mid-step once more. He was moving away from that voice.

He glanced over his shoulder again. Andreas stumbled, his facial expression contorted as he seemed to struggle with something within his mind. Ezekiel wondered if Andreas had heard her voice too. Maybe she called for him as well.

"Zeke," Andreas said, wincing as though pain rocked him, "I think we're going the wrong way. Something feels off. I can't place exactly what though."

Ezekiel faced the light again. He took a step closer to them, and another, eyes glued to the dancing bulbs of blue light. They drew him in, as though a tether was attached to his chest, pulling and tugging, just a little, inch by inch. Enough to keep him moving forward. Closer to the lights. The warm, inviting lights.

He went to take another step, and a gust of air blew over him from below.

"Close your eyes!" Andreas shouted from behind him.

Ezekiel snapped his eyes shut just as he was yanked backward and landed on his ass on the stone floor. In the darkness behind his eyes, he thought about Sophia.

Her face came to him as clearly as looking into glass. She smiled at him, and his whole body reacted.

Firm hands gripped Ezekiel's head, holding him rigid. "Clear your mind, Ezekiel. Can't you hear them whispering?" It was her voice again. The one that called to him.

Sophia's voice was so clear in his mind, he must've been dreaming. Ezekiel concentrated on his breathing, taking in one breath, letting it out, and taking in another. He dug deep into his psyche, reaching for his magic to cleanse him. And he heard it—he heard *them*. The tiny tinkling of one hundred voices twisted into one.

"Come with us. Come with us. Follow us to salvation."

Ezekiel opened his eyes to see his beloved Sophia's beautiful face. "What are they?" he asked.

"Wisps. Remember?" Sophia asked.

He did remember. He was with Edric, Sophia, and Andreas, and they had come upon a mass of wisps blocking their path to the vault. They needed to find the vault, to help Sophia find the heirs to the throne. He'd conducted a smoke spell to snuff out their light. But the spell had, obviously, gone wrong. He and Andreas had somehow been separated from the others, and if it weren't for Sophia calling him back, he'd be lost for good.

SOPHIA

Sophia still had starbursts behind her eyes as she stared at Ezekiel. The wisps' power had taken them by surprise. As far as she could tell, after Ezekiel had conjured the smoke spell to disarm the wisps, the tiny creatures had intensified their light and efforts, luring him and Andreas down another passageway, one that would be their doom. Thankfully, she and Edric were able to shake off the wisps' influence and track the other two men down. Just in time.

She shuddered at the thought of what would have happened to Ezekiel and Andreas if she had shown up just a moment later, barely long enough to take a breath. She had underestimated the wisps, and it had nearly cost her two of her beautiful men. Two of her team. She didn't think she would have been able to survive that loss.

"What happened?" Ezekiel asked, as she helped him to his feet.

"You were almost Zeke kabobs," Andreas said. "If it hadn't been for Sophia, I think we would've both been on spikes."

Sophia turned toward the wisps that still floated nearby, whispering their deadly promises. "Play time is over."

She'd faced them in the woods before. She would

deal with them now, and they weren't going to be happy about it.

Concentrating on pulling up her magic from deep inside, she thought about what she wanted to do to the tiny insect-like creatures. She wanted to swat them like flies. Thinking about that, and only that, she cupped her hands. Within seconds, she felt pressure between her palms. When she opened them, a small whirlwind swirled between them. She pushed her magic toward the cloud of wisps.

The whirlwind grew into a tornado, and the chaotic wind whipped at the wisps, sending them sailing into the ceiling, the walls, and the floor. Like insects, they burst into green mush on impact.

Once finished, she reigned in her magic and faced her men.

"Ew," Ezekiel said. "That's gross."

"Shall we continue?" Sophia rolled her eyes and propped her hands on her hips.

They turned around and made their way back the way they came, hoping to find the entrance to the vault that would lead them to a clear direction to follow in finding the heirs.

At the end of the passageway, there was nothing but a dead end. Frowning, Sophia looked back the way they came. "That can't be. The door has to be here, or why were the wisps guarding this tunnel to begin with?"

The men helped her inspect the rock walls, looking for something—anything—that might resemble a latch or a false front.

"I can sense something is here," she said.

"Me too," Ezekiel said.

She ran her hands along the stone, feeling for anything out of the ordinary. As she smoothed them up and down, they started to glow blue.

Ezekiel stepped closer. "Something's reacting to your magic."

Encouraged, she continued to trace her hands along the rock. She made the shape of a large door. Starting in one corner, she went across then down, across on the bottom, then up. The second she connected the invisible lines together, the outline she'd traced also glowed blue.

She stood back as a door appeared in the wall. Once solidified, it was as if the door had always been there. But it wasn't. The magic that concealed the door had to have been powerful. The idea that someone went to such lengths to ensure the room stayed hidden gave Sophia hope that a clue to the heirs really did reside behind that door. Renewed by the hope of finally finishing the task given to her by the oracles, she reached for the door handle and gave it a turn. The wood creaked as it opened inward. Dust filled her nose and she fought back the urge to sneeze.

"We're looking for anything that points to the

heirs. Anything that can shed light onto what happened to them," she said, as she went straight to the bookshelves. "Or where they were taken to."

While the others opened chests and rooted around through old scrolls and looked at bejeweled goblets and other trinkets, she read over the titles of the tomes. A few of them were on spellcasting. One even mentioned dark magic which she resolved to ask Ezekiel about later. Then she spotted a thick, brown leather book with no title.

Something about it called to her and felt vaguely familiar, but she couldn't place why. She must have been here before, or read these books, or something. Though, she couldn't recall a single memory of her doing so. She pressed her fingers to the spine of the tome and pulled the book from its slot. A flash of memory shot through her mind.

Just a smile. Nothing more.

She wasn't even sure if it was male or female, but the image made her jump back as though she were burned.

"Are you all right?" Edric asked, joining her on her left.

She nodded. "Yes. It's nothing."

Shaking the sensation from her mind and her hands, she refocused. She had a job to do, a mission to fulfill. She reached for the book again and ground her teeth against the onslaught of images of the smiling face, a female face. Once fully pulled from the shelf, she flipped through the book's pages. But it was just another book about the lineage of the royal family. And just like the others, there was no pertinent information about the heirs she sought—no names, or birthdates, or genders. Only a passage about the heirs' births. Sophia found it odd that a book covering royal lineage lacked some of the most important information. It seemed as though whoever wrote the entries, did so fully aware of what was to pass. Someone had wanted the heirs hidden, as if they were a myth or hadn't existed at all.

Setting that book aside, Sophia continued on to the other tomes. But after an hour of searching, she was ready to give up. There was nothing of importance here. Nothing they didn't already know or that Ezekiel's books didn't already tell them. Still, she continued. She would exhaust all options before turning away.

She reached the end of the bookshelf and leaned against it, trying to figure out their next move since they couldn't find what they were looking for here.

A cold draft blew against her face. Frowning, she peered ahead, looking for the source. Maybe there was a hole in the wall that led outside. She held a hand up near the wooden bookshelf, hovering it just a few inches away. Another puff of air blew over her skin.

"I think there's something behind the shelf,"

she said.

Her men joined her.

"Maybe there's a lever to open a secret door." Ezekiel started pulling on the books, looking for a hidden latch.

Edric nudged the sorcerer out of the way, grabbed hold of the bookcase, and yanked it back. The muscles in his arms bulged as his face strained with the focus of pulling on something so massive and heavy. The shelf gave way, revealing a hidden door. Edric and Sophia exchanged glances. She gave him a nod, and he pulled open the hidden door to a crevasse barely big enough to stand upright in. There was no artistry to the hole, just grunt work with a pickaxe and equally as rough in texture to the walls in the tunnels that led them to this room.

Ezekiel conjured a ball of green witchlight. He handed it to her and she nodded in thanks.

Holding the ball of light in front of her to light her way, she stepped into the small room. There was nothing inside, except for something wrapped in cloth, lying on the middle of the floor. She knelt down and gingerly unwrapped the cloth to reveal a stone tablet with sigils carved on the surface.

The script was strange and sprawling, hard to decipher. She wasn't familiar with these markings and had never seen the language. "Zeke, you need to see this," she said.

He stepped to the side and knelt next to her. He ran his fingers along the engraved symbols and said, "I'm pretty sure this is Druid."

Edric frowned. "Druid? There are no Druids in Nighthelm. They are one of the elder races."

"They're not in Nighthelm, you're right," Ezekiel said. "But they are rumored to live in Ripthorn Mountain."

"Do you recognize any of the sigils?" Sophia asked.

He pointed to one with a fancy loop and point. "This one. I'm more than sure that it means royal."

"The heirs are still alive," Edric said, as he looked at each of them. Similar looks of surprise and awe were on Andreas's and Ezekiel's faces.

Sophia nodded, believing that to be true. The heirs had to be alive. The oracles wouldn't have sent her on a futile chase if they weren't. Quiet, thoughtful, her mind racing in different directions with possibilities of who the heirs were, she rewrapped the tablet with the cloth and slid it into the traveling pouch hanging off her belt.

"Looks like we are heading for Ripthorn," she said. "Let's get out of here before someone finds us."

The men agreed. After replacing all the items, and the bookshelf, they left the vault and headed for the inn for a few last-minute items before heading for their new hideout.

CHAPTER FOUR

EDRIC

*A*s dawn broke above the city, painting pink and orange over the early morning sky, the group emerged from the side door of the Metropolis. Edric sucked in a deep breath, thankful to be topside and in the fresh, cool air. Ezekiel cast a cloaking spell over each of them, so they could go through the streets without being seen or harassed by the guard that patrolled and searched for them.

Now that it was dawn, and merchants were coming out of their homes to set up their shops and carts, walking through the city would be difficult despite Ezekiel's spell. As the sun climbed into the sky, more people would flood into the streets, increasing the chance of being bumped into.

As Edric led the group, using the least traversed paths to prevent walking into unsuspecting citizens, he kept glancing at Sophia. She seemed withdrawn. Moving only on impulse. Something happened to her in the vault. She must have seen something, and whatever it was that she experienced, she didn't seem likely to talk about it yet. He hoped she would eventually confide in him. For now, he had to wait and trust she would come to him in time.

After they passed through the merchant square, Edric led them around the corner of a pub he used to frequent before he met Sophia. A guard marched onto the street with a stack of parchments and nails and a hammer. He held up his hand for everyone to stop. Watching the guard unfold one parchment, he noticed the images under a bold "Wanted."

His face, along with Andreas's and Ezekiel's and Sophia's, was plastered across the paper. The guard left, allowing him and the group to move closer, so he could read the declarations. Edric clenched his fists as his eyes scanned the words. The poster was nothing but a smear campaign. Sophia was labeled an *anima contritum*, and he, Andreas, and Ezekiel were listed as her accomplices.

An elderly woman holding a baby approached the board. Edric backed up as she stepped closer and her eyes widened as she read. She shuddered, held the baby closer, and rushed off. The posters were definitely having the desired effect. Sowing and spreading fear among Nighthelm's populace.

"That's going to make it harder for us to do anything in the city," Andreas whispered. "We'll have more than just guards looking for us."

"We're innocent until proven guilty," Edric said.

"These posters say a whole different thing," Ezekiel said. "Not to mention they're working."

"Yes, this will spook the whole city." He looked at Sophia. Worry and guilt filled her eyes. He reached for her hand and gave it a loving squeeze. "You didn't do this, love."

She swallowed. "You're wanted criminals because of me."

Ezekiel touched her cheek. "Hey, I've always wanted to be a criminal. It's more exciting. I was getting tired of doing magic for a bunch of old, doddering fools who never appreciated me." He smiled.

She did the same, but it didn't quite reach her eyes. Edric wanted to pull her in close and hold her until the pain ebbed away. He would have, but he knew she had a purpose and he couldn't let these posters get in the way of her accomplishing her mission. Wanted or not, Edric would be damned if he couldn't help Sophia find the heirs.

"If we're caught, you will all be banished to the mountain," she said. "That's a fate far worse than death."

"Being without you," Edric said, "is a fate worse than death."

Andreas and Ezekiel nodded in agreement.

But she spoke the truth, the punishment for traitors against the realm was banishment to Ripthorn Mountain. The rumors were that humans weren't able to stand the magic of the mountain, seeping into the body and eating everything from the inside out, until the unfortunate soul withered away into nothing. Besides that, the creatures rumored to live in the mountain would be just as horrific to encounter. Edric would face that and so much more if he needed to. Helping Sophia was worth every punishment he would ever face.

His attention was caught by another guard that took station just a short way down the road. He recognized him as an old war buddy and his former guard. Malcolm would have information for them. Maybe even lend a hand. He was trustworthy, and Edric knew he would keep quiet about their meeting.

Turning to Ezekiel, he said, "Get Sophia back to the inn. Andreas and I need to gather intelligence. We need to know exactly what is going on with our people, and what Winston plans to do."

"Got it." Ezekiel nodded.

Sophia grabbed his arm before he could race off. He met her gaze and nearly gave up on the mission in favor of holding her. She reached up and pressed a soft kiss to his lips. She turned to Andreas and did the same.

"Be safe, both of you, and return to me as soon as you can," she said.

Andreas slapped a hand on Edric's back and Ezekiel's shoulder before dissolving into the shadows to meet with his brotherhood in the Shade. Edric stayed glued to the wall until Ezekiel and Sophia slipped down the street and disappeared around the corner. He kept his gaze on the guards milling about to make sure no one had noticed them escape.

Edric moved closer, trying to catch Malcolm's attention. And *only* his attention. Malcolm turned his head toward Edric, who motioned with his hand to keep things quiet. He pushed off the wall and walked across the street, gesturing to the alleyway nearby with a nod of his head. Once within the shadows, he watched as his old friend followed. He looked over his shoulder once before stepping into the alley.

Edric said, "It's good to see you, my friend." They shook hands, clasping each other's wrists.

"The word is you murdered the headmistress," Malcolm said.

"Winston Kent's word, I imagine." Edric narrowed his eyes.

Malcolm nodded. "The little shit is spewing a lot of dangerous things about you and this woman, Sophia.

He says you're trying to destroy Nighthelm, to bring about chaos and anarchy."

Edric snorted and shook his head. "Whatever he's telling you, it's not true." He could only imagine the vile things that bastard spread about him and his companions.

"I know. As do many who are still loyal to you, Commander." Malcolm glanced toward the mouth of the alleyway. "He's got a bunch of mercenaries hunting for you and your friends. He knows a lot of us won't bring you in."

Edric crossed his arms over his chest and placed his feet shoulder-width apart. "What does the duchess say about all of this?"

Malcolm shrugged. "Not saying much, surprisingly. Seems like she's letting him run the show. The Kents have long been supporters of the duchess."

Edric nodded. Though that was true, he had hoped there would have been a bit more reluctance in the duchess. However, that seemed wishful thinking. "Thank you, Malcolm. I won't forget this."

His comrade in arms slammed his fist against his chest. "Warriors of Nighthelm."

"Warriors of Nighthelm." Edric left Malcolm and slid out of the alleyway, heading back to the inn. The long way. He needed to see for himself just how far Winston Kent's hold extended.

Two blocks later, he came dangerously close to the

barracks. He spied armed troops forming into battalions. In his gut, he knew where they were going. Head down, heart pounding, he ran as fast as his legs could move.

∼

ANDREAS

Slipping into the Shade wasn't difficult. The area of the city was devoid of most regular people and the city guards. Only wraiths lived in the Shade. And most wraiths were loyal to the royal family and not the duchess, who was just the steward.

As he walked the streets, he received a couple of cautious looks, but he trusted his people to not rat him out, not unless he gave them a good reason to. Rumors spread by a sniveling worm like Winston Kent wouldn't sway too many in this district.

Ozul grunted when Andreas stepped into the room. "'Bout time you showed back up. How's the new place?"

"Old, smelly, and dilapidated."

"Captain Ryder said you weren't dumb enough to end up back here." Ozul chuckled.

"Is he looking for me?" Andreas asked.

Ozul shook his head. "You know the captain isn't going to do what some human asshole orders him to do." He snorted. "Well, it seems as word is spreading of you and your friends wanting to usurp the duchess and her seat."

Andreas shook his head. "And what do you think?"

Mica handed him a jug of *ouzo*, a thick alcohol that tasted like wildfire, which they made out of grapes and spices. "Is it true your woman is an *anima contritum*?"

Andreas took the jug and tilted it to his mouth. The liquid burned his throat, but it felt good. He wiped his mouth and nodded. "Yes. She's extremely powerful."

"She's dangerous," Ozul said, as he reached for the *ouzo*.

"That too," Andreas agreed, with a smile. He loved how unpredictable and formidable Sophia was. It called to him on many levels. She made him think of the wild nature of the forest and the mountain. She was an outsider, an *other*, just like him.

"There's lots of confusion and fear in the city," Ozul said. "Everyone is looking for you and this woman, the commander, and the sorcerer. You are making everyone nervous."

Andreas took another long pull on the jug. "Are *you*?"

Ozul made a face and waved him off. "Takes more than you and some crazy rumors to make me nervous."

"What have you heard?" Andreas asked.

"That this woman, Sophia, assassinated Headmistress Mittle as well as Professor Grindel while they were trying to cure her. She's cast evil magic on you and the others, talking you into helping her kill the duchess and destroying the city. That if she's not stopped, she will raze the city to ashes and bring the evil of the mountain upon us all."

Andreas nodded slowly. "That's a lot of evil killing going on."

Ozul shrugged. "Humans are easily frightened by things they don't know or understand."

They all knew this better than most. Wraiths were persecuted for years before the king pardoned them all and allowed them to live in the city as equals. Despite all the joint missions together with the city guard, he and his wraith warrior brothers were never treated as equals. Over the years, Andreas had seen the wary looks and heard the snide comments whispered behind his back.

He appreciated he'd never received those looks or heard those comments from Edric or Ezekiel over the years, not even when they were competing over everything. And now, Andreas considered them to be his brothers.

Mica took a long drink of *ouzo* and studied Andreas over the rim of the jug. "Contritums possess mountain magic. We as a people respect the mountain. Your woman has nothing to fear from our people."

Andreas nodded and offered his hand in brotherhood. Mica clasped it while looking him straight in the eyes, as was their custom.

Ozul also shook his hand. "Lay low. Wherever you're hiding, stay there. We'll see what we can do to help."

"Thank you, my brothers."

CHAPTER FIVE
SOPHIA

Sweat trickled down Sophia's back as she dodged the weighted stick coming at her head. She spun around to strike her opponent in the flank with her broad sword, then took two steps back and put her sword at the ready, angling her body with a wide stance and waited for the next attack.

The wooden dummy Ezekiel had made with a few left-over mops and brooms for her to train with in one of the open rooms upstairs, floated back, fully animated. Its padded training stick lifted high in the air as it charged her. She moved to the left and swung her sword up toward the dummy's wooden appendages. If the thing had been a real person, the blow would've taken an arm clean off.

The dummy spun around and came back at her,

sword held low, and she knew exactly how the attack was going to go. The move was telegraphed in the way the dummy's appendages arched. As she took a step back and made a diagonal cut across its body, Grindel's commanding voice echoed in her head.

"Zornhau!"

"Mittelhau!"

"Oberhau!"

Each move he would shout at her, and if she didn't do the motion right, he would make her do it all over again, twice as hard, for twice as long. The pain of his loss stabbed her deeper than any sword.

The dummy recovered from the blow and charged at her again. This time, she lifted her sword over her head and chopped down on top of its non-existent head. Her blade cut through the wood, rendering the whole thing in half. The pieces dropped to the floor with a loud clatter.

Breathing hard, Sophia lowered her sword with shaking arms. She hated being cooped up. If she could just sneak out into the forest and go for a long run, she'd feel so much better. Running her sword through Winston's gut would also make her feel better. But a girl couldn't have everything she desired. That was too greedy. She would be satisfied with just rendering Winston in two.

She sheathed her sword and chugged down the

water that had been left for her in a large mug. She wiped at the sweat on her face, pushing back tendrils of blond hair that had come out of her braid. She probably looked a mess. A long hot bath would do her some good. Maybe she'd find Ezekiel and ask him to join her. She imagined they could both use the release.

Exhausted from her training, but with her mind still buzzing, she returned to the main floor. She wandered into the spacious living room to find Haris trying to get comfortable. Every time he moved, his antlers snagged on something. So far, he'd torn down the chandelier, ripped the wallpaper on the walls, and impaled an expensive, high-backed silk covered chair. After that little accident, Ezekiel had instructed Howard to remove all the furniture from one half of the room for the yakshi. They had brought food and water to him, so he wouldn't have to move around too much. It had worked for a temporary solution, but Sophia knew he wouldn't be happy here. He needed to run, just like she did.

He swung his head toward her when she moved into the room. Chuckling at the tassels stuck in his antlers from the curtain he'd just torn down, she stroked a hand down his flank. "I'm sorry, my friend. I know this is hard for you."

He snorted at her in anger. She knew he wasn't angry *at* her, but at the situation. She was pissed off too. She hated being confined and restrained like this. Her time here felt almost like imprisonment, although she knew her men didn't mean for it to feel like that. They were doing what was best to protect her, and themselves. Still, she had to keep in mind their current situation wouldn't last forever. Though that didn't seem to ease the need for freedom.

Sophia reached up and untangled the golden tassels from his antlers. "You know if we could go to the woods, we would do it in a heartbeat. But it's not safe. Not for me, not for you." She tossed the tassel to the side, then nuzzled her face against his cheek. "I would die if I ever lost you, my friend."

Haris trilled softly and rubbed against her.

"Am I intruding?" Ezekiel asked as he entered the room.

Sophia glanced over her shoulder and shook her head.

"I trust you had a good workout?" His lips twisted upward. He must have gone to check on her there first and saw the results of her workout before coming to her here.

"Sorry for ruining your practice dummy," she said.

He shrugged. "Nothing I can't fix."

She rolled her shoulders. "I'm feeling restless. So is Haris."

The yakshi snorted and rustled his body in agreement.

She sighed and said, "I'm not sure how long either of us can continue to stay locked up inside."

He seemed to think about that for a moment, lips pressed into a line and a crease appeared between his eyebrows. Sophia waited as he worked whatever problem out. Finally, he nodded and said, "I might have a way for Haris to travel with you, almost like a ghost in the ether. It won't help your restlessness, but it may bring you both some comfort."

She moved closer him, trying hard not to bounce like a giddy little girl or those girls in town that swooned over every little thing a handsome man did. "How?"

Haris's ears flicked forward, he was interested as well.

"A fusing rite. I will link his energy—his life force—to you. He'll appear as a tattoo on you. Then you can summon him at will and release him onto this plane as a physical being," Ezekiel said.

She frowned. That sounded horrible and no different than what they were dealing with now. Only Haris would be an image on her body, essentially exchanging one prison for another. The idea seemed cruel in essence. "Where would his life force be when not physically on this plane?"

"In another realm, the ether. There wouldn't be any constraints on him there. He would be able to run free."

Haris got to his feet and huffed loudly, nodding his big head up and down.

Ezekiel smiled. "Seems like he's up for it."

Sophia patted her friend's furry cheek. She still didn't like the idea. Though, it was appealing that he would be in another realm, running free. She stared into her friend's eyes as light and hope shone through them. She asked, "Are you sure?"

He nodded his head again, nearly knocking her over as he did. Haris wanted this. And he would be close enough that she could call on him any time she needed. Maybe this was the best thing for her friend.

"Okay." She nodded to Ezekiel. "Do it."

Ezekiel pointed to the other side of the room. "Could you both move over there?"

Haris walked to the other side of the room, his hooves clacked on the wooden floor. Sophia went with him, nerves shooting through her. She knew Ezekiel would never do anything to hurt her or Haris, but this magic was completely foreign to her. He was a powerful sorcerer, and she'd been on the receiving end of one of his spells, so she knew the level of energy he could use. It was both magnificent and unnerving.

When they were both out of the way, Ezekiel drew out a casting circle in white chalk he pulled from his pocket on the hardwood floor. Sophia couldn't make heads or tails of the symbols he drew, and it was fascinating to watch him work. Once he was finished, he took a step back and studied his design. He nodded to himself and placed the chalk back into his pocket.

"Sophia, please stand here." He pointed to a segment of the circle directly across from him. The symbol reminded her of an hourglass with waving lines above and below it. "Haris, up here." He pointed to another spot directly across from where Sophia stood. She couldn't quite make out the symbol except for what looked like an arrow with a circle around it and a few other symbols on either side.

Once they were positioned, Ezekiel stood in the center of the casting circle, directly between Haris and Sophia. He closed his eyes, rubbed his hands together, and mumbled a few words under his breath. Within moments, a thick, golden rope appeared in his hands.

"Hold out your right arm, Sophia."

She did, and he draped one end of the rope over her forearm and then wound it around her three times. He wrapped the other end of the rope around Haris's thick neck three times. When that was done, Ezekiel grabbed the middle of the rope with both hands.

He glanced at her. "It might hurt a little, and I'm sorry for that."

She gave him a curt nod to proceed. A little pain was nothing compared to giving comfort to Haris.

Ezekiel muttered words in a language she didn't

understand. The arcane language sorcerers use for their spells.

Blue light emanated from Ezekiel's hands. It was faint at first but then swelled into a brighter glow. The light swirled around the rope, cascading outward, spinning faster and faster, until the magic wrapped around Sophia's arm and Haris's neck.

The light intensified, forcing Sophia to turn her face. Haris snorted and stamped his foot. She wanted to reassure him but didn't know if her words would interfere with the spell. Haris wanted this, and the last thing she wanted to do was mess it up unintentionally.

Heat blossomed over her arm, and she winced against the burn. She bit down on her lip to further force back the pain. She would do anything for her yakshi friend. Even endure the pain of one thousand needles if that meant Haris would be happy.

All at once, the light and pain vanished. She opened her eyes and turned her attention to the spot Haris had been standing in. He was no longer there.

Her heart palpitated right as Ezekiel gently gripped her arm and turned it so that her forearm faced her. Taking up her once plain skin was Haris, standing in incredible detail, just like a tattoo. "By the Gods." She let out a long, heavy breath. She traced the outline of Haris with her fingertips. "I can feel him."

Ezekiel said, "He's with you. A part of you now."

A sense of security washed over her, as if Haris was

right at her side, ready to fight at a word's notice. Having him on her arm felt right. And she knew Haris was happy as well. The connection between them had become more concrete with him on her arm. But the question was how she could see him in front of her, summon him at will.

"How do I summon him?" she asked.

"Press your hand over the tattoo and say, *Vocavi*."

Sophia set her hand over Haris's image. "*Vocavi*."

Nothing happened.

She frowned. "Why didn't it work?"

"You have to use your magic. You're more powerful than you think you are, Sophia. I can feel your power humming all around you." He placed his hand close to her face, just hovering above her cheek. A tiny spark ignited between his fingers and her flesh. He shivered, and his eyes darkened and narrowed. Heat blossomed in her gut. She had never seen him react to her in such a way. It was deep, passionate, and the need for her was clear in his eyes.

He cleared his throat and said, "Try again."

Breathing in deep, she placed her left hand over her tattoo and concentrated. She pictured Haris in her mind. His heartbeat returned her touch. Tapping into her magic, she uttered, "*Vocavi*."

The air shimmered, like a view of lights through a glass window with rain drops. Pressure pulled her head and body, as though some invisible force squeezed her too tightly. Green smoke filtered around her fingers, taking shape in front of her. The smoke solidified into Haris's form. He shook his big body, and his antlers scratched along the wooden ceiling. He groaned and lowered his head and stamped his foot twice.

Grinning, she wrapped her arms around his neck. "I can't believe it." She ran her hands over him. "Are you okay?"

He trilled happily and nudged his nose against her face.

She faced Ezekiel and asked, "How do I send him back?"

"Again, touch the tattoo and say, *reverte*." He had the look of awe in his expression. Sophia smiled, feeling rather proud of herself as well.

She turned her gaze to Haris, staring him in his eyes. "Are you ready, my friend?"

He snorted, and she took that as a yes.

She put her hand on her arm, trusting in Ezekiel's magic as well as her own. "*Reverte*."

In much the same way as he appeared, Haris dissolved into green smoke and returned to her arm in the same image as before. Again, the feeling of security and love enveloped her.

She sighed with relief. "Thank you."

"You're welcome." He smiled. "Eventually, you'll be

able to summon him without words, just with your magic and intentions."

She moved to stand in front of him and wrapped her arms around his neck and kissed him hard. At first, he chuckled under her lips, then he buried his hands in her hair and deepened the kiss until she was breathless and wanting more.

CHAPTER SIX

EZEKIEL

Kissing Sophia was like a drug.

It filled him with a heat that burned through his veins in the most addicting and powerful way. He couldn't get enough of kissing her, and he didn't want to. His hands cupped her round firm ass. He moved his hands lower, gripping her thighs and pulling her up. She moaned and wrapped her legs around his waist. His pants grew tighter. As soon as he took a step toward the stairs to carry her to a bed to release his growing need and temper the burning passion between them, Edric burst through the door.

Sophia quickly pulled her lips from his and faced Edric. Ezekiel did the same, albeit with a resentful grudge and a frown. The last thing he wanted to do is leave Sophia in the middle of what they were doing.

But as soon as he set his eyes on Edric, noticing his labored breathing and sweat covered face, that resentment turned to worry.

"Sorry to interrupt. But we're about to be raided. Over seventy troops are heading this way."

Ezekiel set Sophia down and faced Edric. "Did you see any sorcerers with them?" He rushed through the room, making sure his wards were still in place on the windows and doors, adding in extra power and energy to each.

"I don't know," Edric said. "Maybe. There were a couple of men not in uniform."

That could mean they were able to get a capable, powerful sorcerer from outside of Nighthelm faster than expected. Ezekiel thought he would have more time to prepare, to amass magical weapons they were going to need. However, it was more likely that Winston and those he'd been able to sway to embrace his bogus cause were impatient and trying to catch him and his group off guard. Either that, or they had underestimated his power, which was a terrible move on Winston's part.

As Ezekiel checked the ward on the front door, Andreas's black smoke form floated through. He shifted back to his human form and said, "We have a huge problem."

"I know." Ezekiel rushed back into the dining room

where Edric and Sophia were arming up. Andreas followed him.

"I'm going to cast an enchantment that won't allow any intruders to see us, even if they get into the house," he said.

"How did they even find us?" Sophia asked. "And so soon?"

Ezekiel paused in his casting to address her concern. "The amount of power it takes to keep these wards up could be detected by extremely powerful sorcerers. If Winston was able to contact one outside of Nighthelm, it is possible the sorcerer picked up on the enchantments nearby which could have alerted them to our location."

"Or there is a spy," Edric said. "Winston may have swayed some men to his side. He may have had eyes on us the entire time without us being aware of the fact. As careful as we were, I'm afraid we may not have taken everything into consideration."

Andreas unsheathed the blades strapped to his back. "Your enchantment, does it allow us to fight them? Will they be able to feel my steel?"

"You can't interact with them or the spell fails, and you will be seen, which will alert everyone to our presence. That has to be a last resort only. Otherwise, avoid contact at all costs." He made his way toward the bar counter and pulled open a tote he left there, full of his supplies. Pulling out a small jar, he unscrewed the lid then took Edric's arm. Edric tried to pull away, but Ezekiel held firm.

Edric's eyes widened. "Strong grip."

"Thanks," Ezekiel said as he tucked Edric's arm under his, holding it firmly in place as he pulled the sleeve of his shirt up, twisted off the lid of the container, and dipped his finger in the substance, pulling out a dark-green, ink like liquid.

Edric asked, "What are you doing?"

"Hold still." Using his finger covered in the thick substance, he drew a T, a circle above that, an arrow through the straight line of the T, and a small swirl at the bottom. "This will connect us and make you invisible to others. We'll be able to see you, but no one else will."

He drew the same sigil on Sophia and Andreas's forearms.

"Feels weird," Edric said.

Ezekiel looked at Edric, taking in the confused expression that covered his face. He shook his head. "That means it's working."

Shouts echoed from outside. Through the window, Ezekiel saw a stream of men charging toward the inn.

"Andreas and I will take the back," Edric said, and he and Andreas raced out of the room toward the rear entrance of the inn where Ezekiel was certain more soldiers gathered, ready to break in.

A bang knocked at the front door. Ezekiel and

Sophia moved toward it, listening to the voices on the other side.

"There's nothing here," one man said, a solider most likely.

"Just keep swinging that thing. They are here, the inn is just enchanted." That voice belonged to Lewyss, another sorcerer from the castle, and a man Ezekiel didn't like.

Lewyss had always been jealous of Ezekiel and the clout he had earned with those in power. Obviously, that clout hadn't done a single thing, since sorcerers and guards were knocking down his door to arrest him and everyone he cared about. They would likely have them banished to the mountain.

Another loud bang rattled the wooden door. The wood splintered, and a battering ram burst through. Troops swarmed through the shattered door, swords raised and ready. Three sorcerers followed. One of them was Lewyss, and Ezekiel had to tamp down the urge to reach past his enchantment and strangle him. The other two were Palleas and Udal, both of whom he called friends.

Sophia clung to his arm. She gave him a pointed look that said he'd better not. She must have seen the intention in his eyes.

There was another crash from the back of the house, and Ezekiel assumed soldiers had broken down the back door. The sound of at least fifty sets of boots stomping through the inn echoed through the walls, nearly shaking the foundation.

As guards tore apart each room, the three sorcerers stood by and watched. Ezekiel saw the reluctance on Palleas and Udal's faces, and the glee in Lewyss's.

"This is wrong," Palleas said. "Ezekiel has always been a loyal servant of Nighthelm. He would never conspire to destroy it."

"There has to be a reason the duchess would allow this," Udal said.

"She's being influenced by that Winston Kent," Palleas said with a sneer. "Such a boorish man. Who knows what sort of manipulation he's pulled on her."

Lewyss joined the two sorcerers in the living room. "Ezekiel has always been weak, especially around women. I can just imagine how the contritum bitch lured him to her side," Lewyss said. His lecherous grin made Ezekiel's hands clench into fists. "I look forward to taking his place in the castle."

Both Palleas and Udal turned and left the house. Ezekiel appreciated their loyalty and imagined they had been forced to join the raiding party. Winston probably used their loyalty and friendship as a means to hold them accountable for the crimes Winston claimed Ezekiel and his friends had committed.

Traps Ezekiel had set started to go off. An electrical zapping sound here, and a sizzling fire there.

Screams filtered through the rooms and smoke poured through in thick clouds.

Time to go.

Ezekiel grabbed Sophia's hand and started to make their way through the inn to where Andreas and Edric were, so they could collect themselves and leave. As soon as he took a step toward the hall that would lead them to their freedom, Winston Kent stepped into the doorway, looking ever like the distraught little boy who didn't get his favorite Winter's Giving gift he had asked for all year long. His eyes raked right over him and Sophia, jaws clenched and fists tight at his sides. Winston spotted Lewyss and marched right toward him.

The traitor himself conferred with the man who vied for Ezekiel's position as top sorcerer. He seemed positively gleeful at the prospect of replacing him. He forced back a groan.

"The enchantments and wards on the house are strong," Lewyss said. "The best course of action is to burn it all down."

Winston shook his head. "No."

"Why not? It's the best way. Fire will destroy all the wards and enchantments, and if the traitors are still here, it will burn them down too."

"Do the job I'm paying you for and break the wards," Winston barked. "Or you can go back to the castle with your tail between your legs and continue being the bottom feeder that you are."

Lewyss huffed and walked out of the room.

Winston walked through directly in front of them and stopped in the middle of the room, his gaze taking in the casting circle and the grooves that Haris's hooves had made. Squinting, he surveyed the whole room. A small smile crossed his face.

"Sophia will be mine, one way or another," he murmured.

Ezekiel wondered if Winston knew he was there, listening. He must've known they were still in the house, or he would've ordered it all to be razed the ground. Like Lewyss had said, it was the best way to be certain.

Now that Winston was alone, this could be his chance to take him out before he did any more damage. He slowly made his way across the room, careful not to give his position away. Winston was quick with his blade. Ezekiel had watched the man train before, and he didn't want a knife in this throat.

"And those filthy wraiths," Winston said. "Refusing to join me. I'm not surprised, all those beasts are loyal to each other, even traitors."

Sophia crept around Ezekiel, cautiously moving behind Winston. Her hands flexed over her sword and dagger, ready to attack. Tiny sparks sizzled on the tips of her gloved fingers. That was most definitely new. She shifted her gaze to his.

He shook his head and mouthed, "Don't."

She clenched her hands and pressed her lips tightly together. Her shoulders raised with the deep breath she took. She closed her eyes as her lips pursed and her shoulders dropped. The sparks disappeared.

Ezekiel slid his dagger out of its sheath on his belt and took a step closer to Winston. Before he could slide his knife into the man, an explosion rocked the house, knocking him off balance. The trap to his room had gone off. They had little time left before the final trap was found and the entire skeleton of the inn would come crashing down on top of them. Either him, Sophia, Andreas, and Edric would get out of here before that happened, or Winston and his band of people would.

More black smoke billowed through the doorway into the hall. Rapid, uneven thumps rushed down the stairs. Guards ran out, clutching at their eyes, screaming. Some of them were covered in the powder that caused the black smoke. Ezekiel smiled to himself. He was quite proud of that trap. It worked rather well by the looks of the poor bastards that triggered it.

Winston ran past them and was the first out the door. He even pushed aside an injured soldier to get there.

Run, coward, run.

Sophia dropped to the floor, covering Ezekiel's body with hers. He hugged her as the remaining guards streamed out of the house. They had won this round, but barely. Ezekiel would have to repair the damage of the traps and reset them on top of creating stronger wards. Never mind that next time, if there was a next time—he was sure there would be—Winston would return with someone powerful. Someone Ezekiel wouldn't be able to scare away or out-magic. They had to come up with a plan to leave the inn, to leave Nighthelm.

CHAPTER SEVEN
ANDREAS

Andreas accompanied Edric to rendezvous with one of his trusted contacts in the guard. Like shadows in the night, they moved through the city, careful of the added patrols on the streets until they arrived in an alleyway next to an eerily quiet pub. On most nights, lively music and animated conversation poured from the stone building. The propaganda against him and his team achieved the desired effects. They were proclaimed as people to be feared, to be counted among the rumors of darker things and moving shadows lurking at night, ready to seize innocent citizens. And Nighthelm's uncharacteristic silence was evident of the fear the duchess and Winston placed in the people.

They waited a good while before a large man

wearing guard armor stepped into the shadows of the alleyway.

"What's the word, Malcolm?" Edric asked.

He looked deep into the dark behind Edric and said, "You're either a brave man or a stupid one to be out on the streets this night." He glanced toward the street as the sound of armor clanging together grew louder. Mere breaths later, two guards ran past the mouth of the alley. "It's not safe for either of you. Your wanted posters are everywhere."

"We need you to infiltrate the castle and find some information on the heirs. We need names, ages, and if possible, their last known whereabouts."

Malcolm frowned. "The heirs? The heirs are dead. What good would that information be now?"

"We have reason to believe that the heirs are alive," Edric said.

Malcolm shook his head. "Maybe they are. Maybe they aren't. All I know is you and your people need to get out of Nighthelm. Fast." He rubbed at the stubble on his pointed chin. He huffed and looked around again. Once he returned his gaze to Edric and Andreas, he leaned in closer and in a low voice said, "A massive hunt is being organized. One that makes the attack today look like a sparring match. Word is, Winston pulled strings to get Tryce Klatrix here to the city."

Andreas rolled his eyes and groaned. He didn't

have to be a sorcerer or run in their circles to know who Tryce Klatrix was. His name preceded him as the best sorcerer of his time. Not only was he rumored to be powerful, but also ruthless. Andreas could only guess at what Ezekiel would do once he heard the news.

"Everyone within Nighthelm will come for you the moment Tryce arrives," Malcolm said.

"When is he anticipated to arrive?" Edric asked.

Andreas saw the concern on Edric's face. He probably knew more about Tryce than Andreas did, having been commander of the guard and privy to its strategic secrets.

"Within a week. Maybe less. You should be long gone by then."

Edric nodded. Andreas felt the pit of his stomach clench. So soon. Somehow, they will have to find the heirs while on the run from the damning eyes of all of Nighthelm. Sophia would be disappointed for sure. There had to be a way to still restore the heirs and keep their heads, figuratively and literally.

Malcolm's words interrupted Andreas's thoughts. "I'll try to get into the castle for you, but I don't have access to the restricted sections since Winston doesn't trust me." Malcolm snorted. "Smartest thing that man has ever done."

"Be careful," Edric said. "Don't do anything reckless on my behalf."

"Oh, I'm always careful, friend. Although, knowing who to trust has grown increasingly difficult. Especially those within the ranks. Lots of men trying to save their own asses by turning on you. Marlow was particularly pleased to have a chance to take your place as commander."

Edric shook his head and pinched the bridge of his nose. "He always wanted my position. Never let me forget it either. Not very pleasant to be around."

Malcolm snorted. "Yeah, even promising rank and title to whoever joins behind him."

Andreas frowned, disgusted to hear about Edric's own men betraying him, but he kept his mouth shut. It was a human trait he could never understand. Wraiths never turned on each other. Their brotherhood was for life.

Edric shook Malcolm's hand. "Thank you, my friend."

Malcolm then offered his hand to Andreas, who took it.

"If I find anything, I'll send word," Malcolm said. "But if I were you, I would abandon the fruitless quest to find the heirs and get out of Nighthelm before it's too late." He slunk out of the alleyway and out onto the street.

If anyone other than Sophia had been searching for the heirs, Andreas would also think their quest was fruitless. The truth was, they didn't have a lead, and they had no idea how they would survive a trek into the mountain on a wild goose chase for the long-lost heirs. But Andreas believed in Sophia and the wisdom of the oracles. The heirs had to be alive if the oracles were trying to restore them to the throne with Sophia's help.

Faith was a fickle thing, though. It meant believing in something without any evidence. Wraiths grew up with that kind of faith in the royal family. How many times had he been out in the Witch Woods to wait for a messenger from the mountain about the heirs? Too many to count. Andreas's faith was now devoted to Sophia.

When they returned to the inn, Ezekiel already had new, stronger wards up and the air felt thick and heavy when they walked through the invisible wall. Andreas knew only they could enter because Ezekiel would've set the protections to allow him and Edric through. Otherwise, they probably would've walked right into a wall as hard and unyielding as stone.

Once inside, they found Ezekiel hard at work, cleaning up what the guards destroyed, and some of the guards themselves. Andreas didn't even want to think about what he stepped on as he entered the room and was especially grateful that he found himself in Ezekiel's good graces.

"Where's Sophia?" Edric asked.

"Upstairs in a bath. I told her she needed to relax, if

only for an hour." Ezekiel barely looked up from his work as he continued to clean.

Andreas was surprised he'd been able to get Sophia to do that. He suspected if he snuck up the stairs to her room, she would most likely be swinging her sword, training to fight, instead of sitting in a hot bath.

"What did you find out?" Ezekiel asked, as he dipped a rag into the bucket of soapy water he was cleaning with.

"Tryce Klatrix is supposedly on his way to Nighthelm," Andreas said.

Ezekiel wiped his face with the sleeve of his shirt. "I wondered who they would pay to help them."

"Do you know him?" Edric asked.

He nodded with a sigh. His head hung a bit lower as he seemed to stare at a spot in front of him. "I met him once, years ago, during my travels through the country."

"And?" Edric asked.

"I was present when he skinned a siren alive with only his magic." Ezekiel wiped his mouth again. He closed his eyes as a grim line sealed his lips. "Her screams still haunt me."

"That's barbaric," Andreas said.

Ezekiel nodded. "The man has no compassion. I'm not even sure he has any humanity."

"We need to head to the mountain," Edric said. "As soon as possible."

"I'll need time to prepare some tonics to aid us inside the rock. I may need to risk a trip to my estate for some additional supplies. They'll help keep some of the effects at bay, but if we are down there longer than a few days…" He shook his head, not needing to finish the sentence.

They had all heard stories about what happened to people inside the dark magical wilds of the mountain. Those who did manage to get out were never the same. Not only did their bodies wither away to skin and bone, but their minds deteriorated as well. No one had ever been able to fully communicate the truth of what lay inside the cold darkness.

Edric nodded. "We'll deal with it when the time comes. We have to go, it's the only way."

They all knew the trip into the mountain was inevitable. That was where the heirs vanished, and Andreas was sure that was where they would find them again. In the meantime, they needed to pack up and move to another location before they were at this new sorcerer's mercy. As it had been made clear, he didn't have any.

"We need to move," Andreas said.

Edric nodded. "I agree."

"Where?" Ezekiel looked at Andreas. "Would your people take us in?"

Andreas opened his mouth to answer, but Edric spoke up instead. "We can't hide in the Shade." Edric dropped his gaze, away from Andreas. "The castle monitors the district."

Andreas shook his head and started to pace the room. His breathing turned erratic. Of all the nights they had assumed there were eyes on them, there was. No matter what the king did or said, the duchess undid all the work the wraiths had done to prove themselves, and still, it didn't make a difference. They would never be trusted so long as the duchess whispered words of fear among the populace.

"I knew it. I knew the duchess didn't trust us."

Edric held up his hands in surrender, a look of shame in his eyes. "I'm sorry, brother. I wish it wasn't so."

Andreas nodded, knowing full well it hadn't been Edric's decision. He had been following orders. Nothing more.

When the Averell monarchy had been in place, they were never monitored, never persecuted so severely. Trust had been there from the moment the king opened the gates to all the wraith people and allowed them to settle inside the city walls.

There was only one place they could go. And that was the mountain. No one would follow them inside. No one would be crazy enough to do so.

"How fast can you make your potions?" Andreas asked Ezekiel.

"He seemed to think about it for a moment then tapped his thumb against his fingers on one hand. "The soonest I can have the bare minimum prepared with no supply run is tomorrow evening. I can't rush it quicker than that."

"Good. Because we have to leave as soon as possible," Andreas said.

Edric nodded. "Tomorrow night."

There were nods of agreement all around.

"I'll go tell Sophia," Andreas said and turned on his heel to march upstairs to the bathing room. First, of course, he would stop by Sophia's room and make sure she wasn't in fact trying to sneak out or do something on her own.

CHAPTER EIGHT

SOPHIA

As Sophia packed her weapons into her traveling bag, she chuckled to herself. Her men thought she was having a bath, not sitting on the stairs listening to their conversation. She chomped at the bit to leave, fully intending to go into the mountain by herself to fulfill her destiny. She figured it was better this way, since she'd gotten Edric, Andreas, and Ezekiel into enough trouble. They would never be able to go back to their previous lives. Forever, they would be labeled traitors, unless she could find the heirs and restore them to the throne. After that, they could be pardoned for their crimes. The crimes they had committed for her.

Besides, if she were to perish in the mountain, that would be her fate to accept. She couldn't allow harm to befall her men because of her. They may never understand, but she couldn't stand the thought of her men dying slow agonizing deaths by the poisonous mountain magic.

She shoved another one of her knives into the bag, along with her leather wrist bracers to protect her skin from the string of her bow. Her eyes caught the tattoo on her forearm and imagined what Haris would think about what she was doing. Would he think she was running away? Or protecting her men? Maybe it was a little of both.

Andreas chuckled and said, "Going somewhere?"

She didn't turn as Andreas stepped into the room. She wasn't surprised she hadn't heard him approach. He moved as silent as a ghost. They had that in common. And so much more.

Finally, she said, "I can't stay here anymore. It's best I go."

"Best for whom?"

"You. And Edric, and Ezekiel. I've brought you all nothing but trouble." She shoved another pair of leather pants into the bag. They were padded, better suited for climbing over hard terrain. They wouldn't easily rip or tear on rocks or tree branches.

"If you left, I would follow you," he said, as he moved even closer. His voice was calm, yet dark. Soft, yet deep. "To the ends of the world and beyond. Whether you like it or not."

She sighed, knowing full well he would, despite all her protests.

"Edric and Zeke would, too," he added.

That was true. The men she'd chosen were just as stubborn as she was. Albeit occasionally more. She smiled. She knew she couldn't live without her men. She loved them too much.

Andreas pressed into her back. The heat from his body soaked into her, warming her skin. "It's my duty to protect you, Sophia."

She closed her eyes and leaned into him just a little. Smiling, she said, "I can protect myself."

"I know. Probably more than most. Well, definitely more than most. I have yet to meet another woman that could handle a sword as well as you. You even come close to rivaling Edric." He chuckled as he gently squeezed her upper arms. "Just don't tell him I said that."

She giggled and leaned into his comfort a little more.

They were both outsiders within the city they loved and called home. He knew what it was like to be persecuted. To be thought of as an outsider. He understood her on that level. She appreciated that despite hating that he lived under such terms.

"Indulge me. Let me help protect you," he whispered against her neck, sending a pleasant tingle through her body.

With a sigh, she leaned into him even more. His hands slid down her arms, linking his fingers with hers. He pressed a soft kiss under her ear.

"You don't have to do anything by yourself anymore. Not with me around. And I, for one, will never leave your side. None of us will."

"I know." She closed her eyes, angling her head to allow Andreas to nibble at her neck. His loving touch brought her so much comfort and eased the frayed nerves from the stress of living under the weight of the accusations placed on her and her men. She was grateful for him being there for her. For *all* her men.

Even though she'd always gone solo for years, she had a team now. Men she could rely on. Andreas was right. She didn't have to do anything alone anymore. Her men would truly run to the ends of the world for her and not think twice about it. She was grateful for them, thankful to have them with her. They were family—but even moreso, her loves. She felt whole and less broken with them. Without her men, she would be lost, lacking control of her magic and ever on the run from herself more than the world.

He sucked on her earlobe, and need pooled between her thighs. She slid one hand into his hair as his kisses on her neck turned bolder with more heated passion. He moved his hands up her body, caressing her belly and then her breasts. He stroked her nipples through the fabric of her shirt. A groan left her lips. She ached to be touched. Skin on skin.

As though he sensed her need, Andreas pulled at her shirt, lifting it over her head. He tossed the garment to the side and set his hands back on her breasts, circling his fingers over her nipples. She angled her head back to capture his mouth, kissing him hard, tasting his mouth with her tongue. Andreas's hand moved to the ties on her pants. He untied them and slid his fingers under the fabric, massaging her clit that swelled with each stroke.

He buried his fingers inside her. She moaned and bucked against him. Her ass pushed against his hard erection. She wanted him so desperately, she could barely breathe. This was the release she'd longed for since everything had become a chaotic, tangled mess.

Andreas nudged her toward the bed while pulling at her trousers with his hand. He tugged at the leather until it slipped over her ass and down her legs, collecting in a bundle at her feet. He untied and pulled down his own pants, freeing his firm cock. Sophia bit her lip at the sight of him.

So strong and beautiful. Her wraith lover.

She raked her fingers along his torso, from his shoulders to the base of his stomach.

He bent forward and kissed her deeply, pushing her back onto the bed as she pulled her feet free from her pants that surrounded her ankles. His hands explored her body with hungry need, and she clutched at his head as his tongue moved with hers.

His fingers dipped inside her again, sending tingles through her body and bringing the edge of her release forward.

He pulled away, panting for breath and cupping the side of her face as he stared into her eyes with so much depth that it took her own breath away.

"I would be empty if you left, Sophia," Andreas said, emotion clear in his voice. "You're a piece of me now."

She knew that much was true. He held a piece of her soul. He was just as much a part of her as she was a part of him. She smiled and pulled his mouth to hers, kissing him fervently.

He kissed her back and settled himself between her legs. The tip of his cock teased her entry before sliding into her wetness, filling her completely. A moan escaped her mouth. His thrusts were slow at first but picked up pace and force with each movement.

Sophia wrapped her legs around his waist, allowing him to fill her even more. He tucked his arms under hers, gripping her shoulders, digging his fingers into her skin. And she wrapped her arms around him even tighter as her climax drew ever closer.

The release came as she melted into the bed, moaning. Andreas groaned, almost a primal growl as he allowed her to finish her climax before pulling out and forcefully flipping her to her stomach. She got onto her knees, clutching fistfuls of the fur blanket that covered the bed. He ran his fingers along her back, raising goosebumps along her skin. An electric sensation covered her skin.

"Sophia…" His voice was full of awe.

She glanced over her shoulder and saw tiny blue sparks sizzling up her back. Andreas hovered a hand just above her skin, his eyes wide as he watched the sparks move along her skin. She thought the sight was different as well, but that was the least of her concerns.

"Don't stop," she panted. "

Andreas met her gaze and his lips stretched into a wicked smile. As he entered her again, she closed her eyes and surrendered to the moment. To Andreas.

He wrapped his hands around her body, filling his palms with her breasts as he buried himself deep within her. She could hardly breathe with the intensity of emotions and sensations cascading around her like a whirlpool. It almost made her dizzy. She pushed against him with each thrust, and pressure built in her apex.

As he moved, he slid one hand down and flicked at her sensitive clit. She gasped as his fingers made circles against her swollen mound. The pressure increased as her orgasm began to crescendo.

The muscles in her legs tightened, and her breath

hitched in her throat. Release found her and pushed her over the edge of her threshold, into a pool of pleasure, drowning her in every delicious sensation. Everything around her exploded with color, sound, and texture. Her hands glowed blue, and the very air seemed to caress her like a lover.

Andreas's thrusts quickened, until he groaned and collapsed on top of her. Sweat slicked his skin. Once he stilled, he kissed her on the shoulder. "I think you did indeed kill me."

He chuckled as he pulled out of her then lay on his back on the mattress. She softly laughed and curled into him, draping her arm over his torso as she rested her head on his shoulder. He wrapped an arm around her.

She found herself caught in the afterglow of their lovemaking. She sighed, feeling even closer to him. Closer than she thought she could be. In that moment, she knew she could never leave him, Edric, or Ezekiel. They were each fundamental parts of her. She couldn't live without them anymore than she could live without her heart or breath to fill her lungs.

She angled her head to look at him. Tendrils of dark hair stuck to his forehead and cheeks, and there was a completely satisfied grin on his beautiful face. His eyes were focused on a spot on the ceiling before they shifted to catch her stare. She lifted herself up enough to kiss him on the cheek and lay back on his shoulder.

He wrapped an arm around her, his hand making its way back down to her ass. "Give me a minute and we can go again."

She smiled and shook her head. "You're incorrigible." Her lips found their way over his chin and down to his chest. A sound caught her attention, setting her nerves on guard. She waited for the sound to happen again.

It did. Shifting armor. She knew that sound well.

She looked to Andreas. A crease had formed in between his eyebrows and he pulled from her into a sitting position. "I think that second round may have to wait."

"Agreed," she said and sat.

Andreas stood from the bed and started pulling clothes from the floor, handing Sophia hers. They both dressed and prepared for the worst.

CHAPTER NINE

EDRIC

Edric watched as Ezekiel drew a sigil on the doorframe of the back door to the inn with an enchanted potion. With the information he got from Malcolm, it wouldn't be long before there was another attack. And much sooner than later. He knew they didn't have a week, despite what Winston may have told the guards. Winston would have known some of the guards remained loyal to Edric and would relay any information or orders given to the castle guards. Winston was much more cunning than that. He figured Winston had also sent for the sorcerer the moment things went sideways.

Ezekiel marked the other side of the door and hoped Andreas had talked some reason into Sophia. She was likely packing and preparing to head to the mountain on her own. He knew she was extremely stubborn and blamed herself for the problems they now faced, no matter how many times he and the others had told her he would go to the ends of the world for her. She hadn't made him do anything. He wasn't forced into helping her fight the headmistress and the Nameless Master. He fought because he believed in the prophecy the oracles spoke of, and he believed in her.

Edric had been tempted to dash up the stairs to find Sophia, for his own peace of mind, but he trusted Andreas had done what was necessary. So far, the wraith hadn't run back to tell them she had disappeared. Besides, Ezekiel needed his help, even if the sorcerer was too proud to ask.

Ezekiel turned to face him. He dusted his hands off. White and black powder covered his clothes. "That's it. I've reconstructed several traps in all the rooms. If guards get in this time, they won't ever get out."

Edric nodded. "Good." He went to slap Ezekiel on the shoulder just as the entire inn rumbled. The ground beneath their feet shook, nearly knocking Edric off balance. "What was that?"

"Fuck." Ezekiel glowered. "Looks like they got their sorcerer sooner than expected."

Every window in the house imploded, sending thousands of shards of glass flying. Edric took two steps and grabbed Ezekiel, taking him to the ground just as a large piece of glass sliced through the air, a mere inch from impaling the sorcerer through the head.

Another crack resounded throughout the inn like thunder, and every doorframe snapped like twigs from a tree during a storm. The wood splintered, rendering the wards useless.

Ezekiel jumped to his feet. "Follow me."

"What about Sophia?" Edric asked.

"She's with Andreas. He'll protect her."

Edric followed Zeke to a storage room. Booted feet rushed in and traps were triggered. Screams echoed through the air and mini explosions rocked the inn again. Fire popped and crackled followed by the smell of smoke and burning wood and flesh. They crouched low behind the door while the remaining traps on the bottom floor went off. There would be nothing left of the inn after everything was said and done.

Edric reached for the handle of the door and cracked it open enough to peek into the hallway. The guards frantically flapped at themselves, trying to douse the flames that grew and consumed more of them with each futile movement.

Edric closed the door and shook his head. So much death to his comrades for blindly following such a corrupt idiot as Winston Kent.

"The fire will consume them," Ezekiel said.

Edric nodded. "I saw as much. Remind me to never piss you off, Zeke. You can be very scary and ruthless."

He shrugged. "It's us or them. We have to survive to help Sophia find the heirs and clear our names. Unfortunately, your comrades are casualties of an unnecessary war."

Edric wanted to punch the floor, the wall—anything—to release his anger that grew with Winston's incessant need to get to him and his team. He sucked in a deep breath to try and ease his growing need for wringing that bastard's little neck.

Once the last of the traps were set and the screams had lessened, Ezekiel stood and stepped into the hall. Edric followed with a sigh. He followed the sorcerer to the stairs, eyeing the burnt corpses of his fallen comrades as they made their way through the maze of charred wood and other debris.

An eerie blue glow emanated from Ezekiel's hands as he moved further along. His shoulders became rigid as his back straightened and his steps grew heavier.

A loud command echoed to Edric, and he reached for Ezekiel to stop him as more guards flooded through the smoking embers of the inn. They stopped at the center of the room, where Ezekiel had laid an invisible trapping circle. Watching the guards with confused expressions constantly try to step out of the circle and then bouncing back as they hit the invisible walls made Edric force himself to stifle a chuckle. It truly was a sight to see. One guard took a running start a few feet back and ran toward the other side. He slammed hard into the barrier, squishing his face and nose as if his face had hit glass. The loud thump brought a grin to Edric's face.

When everything was said and done, this whole mess behind them, he would confront the soldier and never let him live it down.

The two men ran across the room, avoiding the circle trap. The captured guards shouted as they did.

"Get them!" one guard yelled from inside the invisible trap. He pulled his sword, but the hilt butted up against the invisible wall and he couldn't fully unsheathe the weapon. Not that it would do him any good. He looked to his buddies, frustration marred his expression.

Two guards who'd just run into the room came at Edric and Ezekiel. Edric moved in front of the sorcerer, with his sword raised. He made short work of them both. Their bodies dropped to the ground, blood gushing from gaping gut wounds.

They quickly made their way toward the stairs. Before he and Ezekiel were halfway there, a flash of bright light filled the room, counteracting Ezekiel's spells and traps. The trapped guards were released and faced both Edric and Ezekiel with their hands on their swords. This time, each of them were able to unsheathe their weapons and held them at the ready.

A tall, reedy man with a pointed bald head, long white beard, vivid blue eyes, and hands glowing with magic stepped through the destroyed doorway of the inn. This had to be Tryce Klatrix, the great sorcerer, hired to destroy them. Beside him stood three more guards and Marlow, who had been Edric's second in command. Malcolm had been right, the man looked pleased at the opportunity to take Edric's place. Anger boiled in his gut. To think, men he trusted with his life took the first opportunity to turn on him. He shook his head and pulled on his own weapon.

Marlow sneered. "I've been waiting for this moment for a long time, Axton."

The guards rushed forward, surrounding them. Edric took up a defensive stance, and Ezekiel did too, his hands sparking with power. A dark form swept into the room. Andreas, in all his dark and brutal wraith embodiment, jumped between him and Ezekiel.

Mouth open, the blood-red glow pouring out with a shriek, Andreas enveloped one guard and lifted him into the air, tossing him against the wall. Edric heard his bones snap. The guard's body fell to the floor, broken.

Two arrows whizzed through the room from the stairs, taking down two more soldiers before they could reach Edric and Ezekiel. Edric glanced to his left to see Sophia, armed with her bow, bursting out from the shadows. His heart pounded at the sight of her. He hadn't realized how worried he'd been.

Tryce lifted his hands and fired bolts of white magic toward Edric. Both Ezekiel and Sophia reached for Edric with their magic, constructing a protection shield in front of him. The white bolts bounced off and fizzled to the ground.

With no time to thank them, Edric was thrust into a melee, Marlow at the head, swinging his sword. Edric blocked his blade, and then countered, bringing his sword around to Marlow's flank. The tip of Edric's blade only brushed against the man's metal breastplate, creating sparks. Another guard joined Marlow's side, eyes narrowed with deadly intent.

Edric risked a glance to Ezekiel, who had his hands full with Tryce. White and blue beams of magic bounced off walls and the floor, zipping by Edric and leaving scorch marks everywhere, singeing the hairs on Edric's bare arms. He had to dance out of the way of one errant ray that would have burned a hole through his leg had he not moved.

Marlow charged Edric again with another wide swing of his broad sword. Edric ducked to the left and brought his sword up from an upward swing, slicing the man across the leg between pieces of leather armor. Marlow grunted and stepped back to examine the new cut that would leave an awfully nasty scar. His eyes lifted to Edric and narrowed. He thrust his sword toward Edric's gut. Edric swung his body to the right, twisted to the left, and brought his blade around. It met Marlow's steel. The clang echoed. The hard blow jarred Edric's hands and arms with a painful shock. Edric clenched his teeth, pressing his lips tight, and shuffled back a few steps to attack again. The tight quarters made every move twice as difficult.

Movement in his periphery caught his attention and he shifted his gaze to Sophia. She fought with her sword now. Two guards advanced on her. They had her pinned against the staircase with nowhere to retreat. But he knew she would fight her way out. She had more skill than most of the men in his unit.

Marlow shouted, "Kill the bitch!"

Several guards charged toward Sophia. Edric ran after them. He cut one down by chopping at his legs, but two more seemed to appear out of nowhere to take his place. There were too many, swarming from all directions and all at once.

Before he could take out another guard, Winston rushed into the inn with several more guards on his tail. They carried something between them. Winston ran toward Edric and the guards and Sophia.

"No!" Winston yelled. "Do not kill her!" He swung at one of his own men in front of him with his sword and cut open his belly.

Edric saw an opportunity to take the traitor out and charged forward. Before he could reach the lying bastard, he took a heavy blow to the flank. He faltered to the side, and the wind was knocked from his lungs. He turned just as Marlow hit him again with a flail. Thankfully, the swinging metal ball didn't have spikes. Although, the weapon had enough force to knock Edric to the ground. He took in a deep breath and winced as sharp pain stabbed through his chest. Some of his ribs were broken with the impact.

Winston stood over him with the pointed tip of his sword pressed into Edric's neck. "If you know what's good for you, and her," he nodded toward Sophia, "You will stay down."

Sophia let out an angry war cry and fought her way out of the corner she'd been pressed into, slicing down man after man. Edric realized she was trying to make her way to him. He didn't have the heart to tell her to stop. Not that she would listen anyway. She was stubborn and standing up for what she felt was right—which meant she would never stand down.

"Capture the wraith," Winston commanded to the guards that accompanied him.

Edric watched as they nodded and moved to where Andreas fought off guards from his corner of the small room. He had busied himself with slicing and clawing at faces and body parts. He didn't see them coming. As the four men moved, spreading out from each other, Edric recognized they held a net in their hands, spreading it out as they moved closer. Each end held a weighted ball made of steel.

"Zeke!" Edric yelled. "Help Andreas."

Winston shoved the pointed sword into Edric's throat, piercing his skin with a burning sensation. "Not another word, or I'll run you through," he said.

Ezekiel still heard and turned his attention toward the men moving in on the wraith. He formed a ball of blue light in this hand and prepared to throw it at the guards with the net, but he was too late. They rushed to close the gap, tossing the net over Andreas. Although his wraith form was made of dark swirling smoke, Andreas still had physical form. The net brought him down hard to the floor, the weighted, steel balls held him firm. All he could do was wiggle and writhe under the weight of the net. He shifted back to his human from. The guards that captured him held their swords pointed at him in case he tried to escape.

"I'm going to kill you!" Sophia shrieked as she cut through another two men to advance on Winston.

Watching her rage tore at Edric's heart. She fought a fruitless battle. Ezekiel dropped to his knees, his hand going to his throat. The other sorcerer clenched his fist, brilliant, white light exploding from it.

They were defeated.

Sophia screamed, "No!"

"Surrender, Sophia," Winston said. "It's over." He

held firm, lips pressed into a grim line and nodded at her. To prove his point further, he added pressure to his sword, forcing the tip a little more into Edric's neck. He winced and tried to pull away from the blade, but the wall wouldn't give.

The expression on her face as she realized there was no way out for them tore at Edric's heart. The feeling was like someone had punched through his chest and clenched his heart to keep it from beating. He'd failed to keep her safe. To keep them *all* safe. He had to make it right somehow. But their situation was dire and there didn't seem to be any other way out of this. He couldn't even reassure her that this was not her fault, though he knew even his words would do little in the way of comforting her.

She lowered her sword, resignation in her expression. Two guards quickly moved in and grabbed her arms. They dragged her toward him and Winston. Winston sheathed his sword and waved a hand toward Tryce. Edric rubbed at the spot on his neck, pulling back blood-tinged fingers. It wasn't a deep cut, but definitely enough to make Edric want to kill Winston all the more.

"Don't kill the sorcerer," he said.

Tryce dropped his fist, and Ezekiel slumped forward onto his hands and took in several deep breaths. He coughed and rubbed at his neck to soothe the ache that must have been there.

Winston smiled, gloating at his victory. "Planning this entire dance wasn't easy, you know. There were quite a few men who didn't want to play along."

Edric knew he spoke about the men who remained loyal to him. Men like Malcolm.

"But they changed their minds after a few hours of…" He smiled again. "Let's say, rigorous conditioning."

Torture. That's what the asshole meant.

Edric stared coldly at Winston and said, "You're a sniveling coward, Kent. Without all these men behind you, you would be absolutely nothing, and I would have my knife through *your* throat."

"Yes, but I still won, and you're going to be dead soon enough." He nodded toward Marlow.

Edric received a hard blow to the side of his head, and everything went black.

CHAPTER TEN

SOPHIA

Sophia yanked at the chains holding her against the stone wall, forced to watch five soldiers holding Andreas as Winston slid a needle into his arm and injected him. She assumed it was hemlock, so he couldn't shift into his wraith form. That had worked so well the last time they were caught in a similar predicament, only that had been due to the headmistress. And Winston would share Mittle's fate—Sophia was going to kill him for that and so much more. She couldn't reach her love. The steel was too strong, and she was too far away. They had purposely chained her to the wall by the wrists and ankles on the opposite side of the prison cell from where they had chained up her men. This way, she could watch every cruel thing done to them, like dosing Andreas with hemlock.

He struggled against their hold and managed to kick one guard in the face before they secured his ankles and broke his nose. But there were too many of them, and he'd already started to suffer the effects of the hemlock coursing through his veins, weakening him.

Ezekiel was chained with his arms strapped wide apart, and by the sigil on the metal cuffs, Sophia assumed he was under some sort of enchantment that prevented him from being able to use his magic. All he could do was watch, sagging against the stone, defeat making his face hard. Sophia hated seeing him so broken.

Edric had been dragged into the room unconscious and was just starting to come around. He shook his head and tried to get to his feet, leaning heavily against the stone wall. "You're going to regret this," he said, his voice calm and measured, cold as ice. "When I get out of these chains, I'm going to kill every single one of you."

The four guards, who hadn't been kicked by Andreas, stepped away, their gazes flitting everywhere but in Edric's direction. Sophia saw the fear on their faces as she memorized each and every single one of them. They should be afraid. Because she would help Edric gut them like pigs the moment they got free.

Once finished with drugging Andreas, Winston

quickly moved back, out of striking distance, and handed the needle to one of the guards. "Leave us."

The guards left quickly and without question. The last one shut the prison door behind him. The audible locking sound reverberated against the stone and echoed in Sophia's ears.

With a final glance at the door, Winston paced the room, letting his eyes settle on each of them as though he were inspecting stock for a banquet.

"I can't tell you how many times I dreamed of this day," Winston said, as he stopped near Edric. "I was promoted just for this occasion. Did you know that? I considered asking for your old job, but I want to go higher than a mere commander. The duchess likes me, so one day soon, I'll even replace my father as general."

"My men won't follow you," Edric said. "They will never follow a half-cocked, traitorous asshole like you."

"Yes, I know, that's why they are all either dead or rotting in one of these cells." He shrugged. It may have been a small matter to him, but those men meant so much more to Edric. Sophia knew that meaning. She understood how much his men mattered to him. She tugged at the chains again, hoping to loosen the plate in the stone wall.

Edric also pulled at his chains, which caused Winston to jump back. Sophia smiled at that. He was such a coward, frightened of her men, even when they were chained up.

He turned and took a couple of steps toward her. His gaze traveled from her feet to her head. She forced back the shiver that his greedy eyes gave her. His hand went to the hilt of the sword he carried, and he pulled it from the sheath. The King's Sword. The one the oracles had given *her*.

Damned thief.

Winston lifted it up, inspecting the weapon. "Beautiful blade. I took this for safe keeping." He leered at her from over the sword. "I still have high hopes for you, dear Sophia."

She rolled her eyes.

He sheathed the sword and took out her dagger from his belt. The gift from Grindel. She gritted her teeth and clenched her hands, imagining wrapping them around Winston's neck and strangling him to death. But that would be too merciful of a way for him to die. He was lucky she still wore her gloves and that her magic didn't burst out of her with a mind of its own.

"The inlay work on this one is extraordinary." He held it up to the meager light provided by flickering torches on the wall. "The old man gave this to you, didn't he?" He sneered. "Too bad he's dead. I think I'll hang on to this one as well."

Sophia yanked at her chains. The metal cuff dug

into her wrists. "I'm going to cut out your eyes with that dagger."

"I'm just hanging onto it until you're better." He smiled and winked.

She frowned, forcing back the urge to vomit. *Better? What does he mean by that?*

He swiveled on his heel, sheathed the dagger on his belt, and walked in front of her men. Andreas struggled with his chains, pulling at them so hard that blood ran down his arms where the metal cut into him.

"I would save your strength, if I were you, wraith. You'll need it when you're banished to the mountain."

Andreas glanced at Ezekiel and Edric.

Winston chuckled. "That's right. After the trial, the three of you will be sent to the mountain." He turned and smiled at Sophia. "While darling Sophia, here, is sentenced to death."

"You bastard," Edric said. Zeke and Andreas fought against their chains.

Winston faced them again and watched as he got some sort of sick enjoyment out of seeing the men struggle against their bonds. "Oh, you don't have to worry. You see, I'll have her locked in a cell for years to rehabilitate her. I'm doing this as a service. Waste not, want not."

A knock rapped at the cell door. Metal clicked, and it opened. Winston turned as the sorcerer, Tryce, walked in. His long blue robes trailing behind him made him look like royalty.

"Ah, yes." Winston moved toward Andreas, pointing a perfectly manicured finger at him. "He's the one."

Ezekiel came to life, pulling at his chains. "What are you going to do?"

"Just a little insurance that the wraith gets what's coming to him," Winston said.

Tryce stood in front of Andreas, calm as he could be. There was no emotion on his face. In fact, his expression was like stone. Sophia forced back a gulp as she had only heard rumors of this famed sorcerer until he showed up with the intent to kill earlier. He reached under his robe and pulled out a small vial filled with a dark liquid and a quill. He nodded to Winston, who rushed over and grabbed hold of Andreas's arm. The same arm he had just injected hemlock into.

Andreas tried to pull away, but Winston proved too strong, seeming to easily hold his arm in a vice grip. Sophia knew it was only because Andreas had already been weakened by the hemlock. He even looked pale, almost sickly.

The sorcerer mumbled words under his breath. She couldn't make them out, but by Ezekiel's pained expression, they were bringing about something harmful. Tryce then dipped the quill into the vial and drew a sigil onto Andreas's forearm. From the distance, she couldn't make out what the symbol was. She probably wouldn't be able to identify it anyway, as she wasn't proficient in sigil magic. Still, Ezekiel's expression turned sour and he shook his head.

Yup, it was bad. And Sophia added Tryce onto her hit list.

When Tryce finished, he took a step back and spat on Andreas's arm. That was when Sophia knew Andreas had been cursed. The many books she was forced to read throughout the years spoke of curses ending with the disdain and intent of the giver. Often times, the curse was sealed with spit, and nothing could undo the ill-fated spell except the caster himself. As far as she could remember, that had never happened. At least, according to her books, anyway.

"Thank you, Tryce," Winston said. "You will be greatly rewarded for your service. You could have the Wickham estate if you wanted." Winston sneered at Ezekiel.

Tryce nodded to Winston but said nothing. He moved silently to the door and left without so much as a backward glance.

"What happened, what did that sorcerer do?" Sophia asked, looking at Ezekiel.

Ezekiel sighed, and shook his head. "Vexsnare curse."

Sophia gasped. Grindel had taught her about the

beasts that lived in the woods and in the mountain. Many she'd come to know, and they weren't as rabid as people claimed them to be. But vexsnares were something different. She'd never seen a vexsnare, as they lived in the mountain, and she was glad for it. They were said to be four-legged beasts with a wolf's head and snakes for a mane, with bony spikes lining their backs. Vexsnares were fierce trackers and could hunt their prey for months over miles of terrain. They also had a healthy appetite for wraiths and had been one of the reasons the wraiths had fled the mountain.

"For the gods' sake, Winston," Sophia said. "What do you hope to get out of doing this?"

He took a few steps toward her, and she wanted to back further into the wall. The last thing she wanted was his filthy body inching nearer to her, and he seemed to get a kick out of making her squirm. The way he gloated over what he'd done made her sick. She had to force back the urge to spit on him. The last thing she wanted was to provoke him when he currently had the upper hand.

"You, Sophia. I want you."

Never. Disgusting asshole.

"No matter what you do, my body would have to be dead and rotting before you could ever have me. And Gods willing, not even then."

He snatched her around the neck and ground his

lips against hers. She bit his lip. Hard. His blood filled her mouth.

He pulled back, stumbling away, and wiped at his lips. Blood coated the back of his hand. She grinned at him.

"When these men are gone, and you are alone, you'll realize I'm the best you'll ever get. That we were made for each other."

"Never." She spat at his feet. "I'll die first."

"You would be surprised what kind of enchantments and talismans I can buy that will make you obedient and *mine*. Even spells that could bring you back from the dead." He grinned again, and she felt the last of her resolve starting to crack.

CHAPTER ELEVEN

SOPHIA

Sophia and her men stood in the center of a circular floor bound by chains dangling from their ankles and wrists. All around them were empty seats. Seats that should've been filled with Nighthelm's populace, jury, magistrates, and council. Only a group of about twenty guards, one magistrate, the duchess, and Winston were present for the trial. And the silence was so thick that every movement and shuffle of their chains or clothing seemed to echo and carry too much volume.

The magistrate seemed anxious, bristling with each clink of the chains. Almost like the noise was painful to him. The duchess watched quietly from her seat, though she seemed rather unnerved by Sophia. It was evident in the way that she wouldn't let her gaze settle on her as long as it settled on the men. She seemed rigid, but Sophia knew it was all a show. Everything about that woman was for show.

And Winston? He looked just as proud and full of himself as ever. Bile rose in Sophia's throat, and she made every effort to ignore his constant smirk as he kept his eyes glued to her. She risked a glance to her men, each of them holding the same puzzled expression as she knew her face betrayed.

For a trial, something felt… off.

She wondered if the citizens of the city were aware that they were being held in a one-sided trial. If so, did they even care? Probably not. More than likely, they were thankful that they could sleep a little more soundly in their beds now.

The wraiths stood outside of the trial room, angrily calling for their right to attend the meeting. Andreas' jaws clenched as Sophia looked to him. She could tell that Andreas didn't like his brothers being kept out and the even more unsettling idea that no one else was allowed in.

A man, no taller than Sophia, entered the room from one of the three doors that led into the room and approached the magistrate's seat of power. It was the door that led directly into the castle's main hall, where the duchess came from. She had been the last to enter.

"Your Honor, the wraiths demand that you reconsider the citizens of Nighthelm's ban from attending the trial." His voice was softer than she thought a man's voice should be, but then, perhaps, he was afraid of the fate that her and her men were about to be given. Or maybe just afraid of the so-called monsters that stood within his presence.

Sophia bit the inside of her cheek. If he only knew it wasn't them that were the monsters. Quite the opposite, really. She exhaled a heavy breath. No use in arguing that now. She needed to focus on how they were going to get out of this mess first. The rest would come later.

The magistrate's powdered wig shook with his head, lips pressed into a tight line. "No audience. The wraiths especially. Their blind loyalty will cause more problems. No one may enter." His voice held a rasp and was worn with age but was also firm with conviction.

But that wasn't right. That's not how the people delivered justice. And Sophia knew it from all the lectures Grindel had given her over the years. She realized that this wasn't a trial. This was for the sake of appearances. Their fates had already been determined. No one would be allowed to speak on their behalf and ask for reconsideration or more leniency.

She didn't have to hear the words to know that they were sentenced to death.

Guilt rocked her core. Kill her, fine. But not her men. She hated that she had gotten them into this mess. It wasn't fair, and now she had to figure out some way to save them. But before she tipped off the guard, much less the magistrate or duchess of her pending plan, she had to come up with the *how*.

"I will now call for order," the magistrate said.

"Then let the people in. Let them come and have a say," Edric said.

Ezekiel added, "Even I know what you are doing is wrong, Your Honor."

"Wrong?" the magistrate asked, stone-grey eyes narrowing on the four of them. "Wrong? Young man, do you not understand the charges and evidence that has been brought against you?"

Ezekiel recoiled. Sophia clamped her mouth shut and glared at the duchess and Winston. What possible evidence could they have to prove any of the accusations? Fabricated ones, that's what.

The magistrate continued. "The way I see it, you are in no position to even so much as speak. You will stand there and accept your conviction, or I will see to it that each of you are gagged." He took several moments to settle his eyes on each of them, pointedly, waiting for another outburst or sign of backtalk so he could deliver on his promise.

Once satisfied that no one else would speak against him and his authority, he said, "The accused, Andreas Hylt, Ezekiel Wickham, and Edric Axton, are all charged with treason, and conspiracy to commit murder."

Ezekiel sneered. "You can only commit treason against the crown." He gestured to the duchess, his chains rattling. "She is not the crown. She is but a steward of the city."

The magistrate twisted his lips into a very unbecoming smirk and pointed at him. "Not one more word out of you." Adjusting his position in his chair, he cleared his throat and continued. "The punishment for these crimes is death."

"No!" Sophia jolted forward, chains dragging on the floor. Two guards jumped toward her and grabbed her arms before she could move any closer to the magistrate. They dragged her back into her place and held her there. Her heart slammed in her chest as she frantically sought for a way out of this mess. A way for her to save her men so that they might continue to live and find the heirs before anyone else suffered from the corruption under the guise of the crown.

"However, seeing that the three men in question had been exceptionally outstanding and law-abiding citizens, serving the city faithfully for many years until being held captive by the enchantments this woman had placed on them, I have reason to believe they acted upon their crimes unwittingly and without control of themselves."

The men shook their heads and opened their mouths to protest, but the magistrate had made a gesture with his hand and at least half of the remaining guards lined up in front of them and held their swords, tips pointed dangerously toward them. "Andreas Hylt, Ezekiel Wickham, Edric Axton, because of your history and service with the city, your penalty has been reduced to banishment," the magistrate said. "To be carried out immediately. Let this be an example for the remaining populace."

That meant they were getting sent to the mountain. That was the same as death. What game they thought they played to make that a sentence, she couldn't figure out. But she would be damned if she allowed her men to go there.

The magistrate continued, "You, Sophia, of no family name, have been charged with being an *anima contritum*. Your sentence is death."

Sophia's breath left her lungs in a whoosh. The rest of the magistrate's words were too muddled to hear as her heartbeats pulsed loudly in her ears. She knew this day would come, but she had hoped that the heirs would have been found and returned to their rightful place in Nighthelm. Her men were to be banished to the mountain, to wither away and die the most agonizing, painful deaths.

Reduction in punishment, my ass.

And to make matters worse, it was all her fault. She had brought them to this fate. Before she died, she would first save them.

Winston smiled at what the magistrate had said

and rubbed his hands together, staring at Sophia like she was his meal. The words he spoke reiterated through her mind…

You would be surprised what kind of enchantments and talismans I can buy that will make you obedient and mine. Even spells that could bring you back from the dead…

His grin widened as her eyes flitted toward him. Almost as if he knew the very words that played through her mind.

Not. Gonna. Happen.

She needed a plan—and fast.

The magistrate nodded and said, "Carry out the orders."

The guards with their swords pointed at the men held firm as two each took Andreas's, Ezekiel's, and Edric's arms, leading them to a stone banishing well etched into the wall to their side. Each of her men glanced at her as they walked past. She saw the looks of fury and loss on their faces, and it was like a knife cut deep into her heart. She couldn't let them go. She wouldn't.

She struggled against her chains and the grip of the guards that held her. Their hands tightened around her arms and she winced from the pressure. As her men drew closer to the well, her entire body started to shake. Heat swelled inside her, like being burned from the inside out. She knew that sensation, she clutched to it, encouraging it to grow.

Clamping her eyes shut, she gritted her teeth until a copper taste coated her tongue. Sophia reached down deep into her body and grabbed hold of her magic. It swirled in her grasp, eager to be released, eager to obey her. Finally.

A collective gasp filled her ears, and she opened her eyes. The two guards that held onto her released her arms and stepped back, eyes wide with fear.

Good.

She glanced down at her hands and saw the blue glow on her skin peeking out from the gloves. She concentrated on that until the metal of her cuffs cracked and shattered like fragile glass, and her hands were free.

Jumping into action, she drew the sword of the guard to her left, then swung at the one to her right, slicing open his torso. His guts slithered out as he clutched at them, trying to keep them from tumbling to the floor. She ran toward the well, just as Andreas reached the hold and was kicked into it.

With a guttural shout, Sophia pushed through the guards descending on her, slicing and hacking at them with her sword, until she made a clear path. Some saw her moves and tried to parry, but they ended up losing a finger, hand, or an entire arm in the process. The magistrate screamed for order and demanded that she be apprehended, but she refused to let her men die for her.

Once she had a way through the guards, she sprinted as hard as she could, reaching for Edric who was the last to be shoved into the well. His eyes widened as he fell, and he shouted her name.

Determined to protect her team, the men she loved—her family—she tossed the stolen sword to the side and dove head first into the gaping hole.

CHAPTER TWELVE

SOPHIA

The hole she dove into started out straight then seemed to bend and twist as she tumbled through. A light appeared, small at first, toward the end. As it grew larger, she realized she would fall through the air before meeting a very rough and sudden stop. And when she did, the drop ended abruptly with her slamming into one of her men and tumbling to the ground as beads of rocks and pebbles dug into her skin, burning with the sting of salt.

Ezekiel conjured a light, illuminating the darkened cave.

Andreas helped her to her feet, and he, along with Edric and Ezekiel, checked her for injuries.

"I'm fine," she said and surveyed each of her men for injuries of their own. Beyond a few unavoidable scrapes and cuts, they looked well.

"Why, Sophia?" Edric asked, a painful expression darkening his features. "Why did you follow us?"

She shook her head and bit her lip. Her heart pounded as the reason why filled her entire being. Because she couldn't let them go. Because she couldn't let them die. She had to follow them. She had no other choice. If she was going to die, then damn it all, she would die with her men at her side. But she escaped that fate, and now her focus was to get her men out before the magic of the mountain drained all the life from them.

She could have said those words, but the pain and relief that filled her wouldn't let her mouth do the work. Instead, she just stood there hoping that her presence alone would be enough of an answer.

Edric approached her and wrapped her tightly in his arms. He breathed in the scent of her hair and placed a tender kiss on the top of her forehead. "You shouldn't have followed us," he murmured into her hair. "But I'm glad you did."

She breathed in his scent and clutched him closer to her. "I had to." Her voice cracked, and she blinked against the sting of tears nipping at her eyes.

"Well I, for one, am glad she did," Andreas said.

Edric pulled from Sophia. Ezekiel stepped forth and took Sophia's hand, gently kissing the top of her gloved knuckles. "I am relieved you are with us as well," he said.

She smiled, relieved that her men were intact and happy she threw herself into the banishing well to come after them. Her eyes took stock of their surroundings, finding bits of roots sticking out from the cave wall. The ground was scattered with skeletal limbs, and huge claw marks left gouges beneath the hole they had just fallen out of. Sophia didn't know what creature had made such marks, but she was glad that the creature hadn't been able to make the more than a ten-foot jump to get there.

"Well, this wasn't exactly how I planned the trip," Ezekiel said. "Now what?"

"We go back," Sophia said. "Before any of us start experiencing the effects of the mountain magic."

Edric said, "You want to go back?" It came out disbelieving.

She nodded. "We need the right equipment, potions to stave off the magic, and our weapons."

Andreas said, "Agreed. May also be a good idea to stop by the Shade to let my people know we are okay."

Edric shook his head. "No. Let everyone think we are dead for the time being. The less anyone knows, the better, and I can't trust that someone won't be on the lookout for something like that."

Sophia said, "That's a good point."

Andreas muttered something under his breath. He stared at a spot on the ground and ran a hand through his hair. Nodding, he said, "Fair enough. So, how do you propose we get out of here?"

Sophia pointed at the claw marks, "See those?"

The men's gazes followed to where she was pointing. Ezekiel drew closer with the ball of light to better examine the markings.

She continued. "There are no skeletons here that would match anything that made those. That means there is a way out of here."

Andreas nodded then shifted to shadow, but he seemed too low to the ground. He tried to move but looked more like the weight of sludge sliding down a stone pipe more than smoke floating weightlessly through the air. He shifted back and shook his head. "Wherever the opening is, I can't move in my wraith form to find it."

"That means the magic is already working," Ezekiel said.

Sophia crossed her arms over her chest. "Either that, or the hemlock has yet to fully leave his system."

"Whatever the reason," Edric said, "we still need to figure out a way out of here."

"Well we can't get out the same way we came in. I can shift, but I can barely carry myself much less anyone else," Andreas said.

"Zeke, how many of those lights can you make?" Edric asked.

He smiled. "As many as necessary." To prove his

point, he created a witchlight for each of them and passed them off one by one.

"Thanks," Sophia said as Ezekiel handed her one.

Zeke winked and smiled.

The room's glow grew brighter and illuminated the small alcove that led to a cavern toward the very back of the cave. It was marked by similar gouges as on the wall.

"There," Sophia said and pointed, "I bet we get out through there."

"Better than staying here to rot and die like these poor bastards," Andreas said and took the first step toward the opening. Edric, followed by Ezekiel, went next. Sophia waited, shifting her ball of light around her to make sure that whatever creature had made those marks wasn't lurking within the shadows, waiting to catch her and her group off guard. Satisfied after observing the absence of anything but her and the men, she followed after them.

After a few quiet moments, Edric said, "Once we leave this area, we'll need to locate a scout to get us the rest of the way home."

"Maybe we could find some information about the heirs while we are here too, as long as we are here and have the strength," Ezekiel said.

"The headmistress said Sophia was found here as well, perhaps there is someone who could give us some more answers as to why?"

"Answers would be nice," Sophia said. "Especially if we are to take out the Nameless Master."

"Know thy enemy," Edric said.

"Exactly," Sophia said, knowing that she kept a mental list of several.

CHAPTER THIRTEEN

ANDREAS

Though his people were from the mountain originally, Andreas could still feel the weight of the magic seeping through his pores, strengthening him. If it affected him this much, he could only imagine what the other three were feeling. Sweat started to bead down his forehead as the tunnel they walked through warmed. It seemed they were climbing higher, deeper into the mountain, rather than out. But he kept his thoughts to himself for the moment. There was still hope that it would lead them to fresh air instead of dank earth and rock.

After a short while, more light penetrated the tunnel. The opening they walked through widened more, and the smell of water filled his nose along with a breeze that gently blew toward him. Relief filled him. The sooner they were out of the mountain, the better they would feel.

Another smell blew into him, and he covered his nose, stopping in his tracks.

"What is that smell?" Edric asked, keeping his voice low.

"I don't know, but I have a bad feeling about this," Andreas said.

Sophia joined his side, mouth twisted down. "Let's take the rest of the way out of here slowly. The opening shouldn't be too much farther. I think we should also extinguish the lights."

Edric nodded. "Agreed."

Ezekiel muttered a single word and the lights all dimmed until there was nothing left.

It took a few moments for Andreas's eyes to adjust to the new dark, but as soon as they did, he noted a light up ahead. He pointed. "That's the exit."

Everyone nodded, and he made a move toward the opening. Just before they reached their freedom, a loud, bone-chilling roar echoed from nearby.

This wasn't good. They didn't have weapons and he was next to useless in his wraith form. Still, they could probably sneak past the creature without being detected. At this point, they really didn't have another choice. If cornered by the creature—from the sound of it, a massive creature—they would likely perish. That wasn't an option.

But what Andreas didn't count on was the mass of cracked earth, as far as the eyes could see, straight in front of him and a massive cliff to the right of that. To his left stood a grove of trees, but it was too far away. The creature's form emerged and drew closer to where they stood, charging at an alarming rate.

"What in the gods' names is that?" Ezekiel asked.

"I don't know, but it looks angry," Andreas said.

"Or hungry," Edric added.

"Either way, we have no choice," Sophia said. "We'll have to fight that thing."

So be it.

Once the creature was close enough for its features to be discerned, it baffled Andreas as to what it could be. It had the head and body of a lion, but the face was humanoid in nature, save for the rows of sharp teeth that protruded from its bottom jaw. And a scorpion's tail was poised and ready to strike them down. It skidded to a stop a few feet in front of them. The beast faced them, pacing back and forth, snapping and growling, dripping saliva from its malformed maw.

Andreas shifted into his wraith form. Whatever this creature was, he wasn't going down without a fight. As he shifted, Ezekiel started muttering some sort of spell or curse. Edric stood in front of Sophia. She scoffed and took a stand next to him, her gloved hands glowing with magic.

Andreas turned his attention to the creature as it

lowered itself in such a way that it looked like a cat ready to pounce on its next meal. It sniffed and shook its head, then sniffed again like it could smell the blood. Its nose drifted from Andreas to Sophia, sniffing toward each of them. Then it stopped and sniffed more at Sophia and growled.

"Magic," the creature said in a blood-chilling voice. "Delicious magic of Ripthorn."

There was no time to react.

The creature lunged toward Sophia.

Andreas rushed toward them, feeling less weighed down. His initial feelings in his form must have been an after effect of the hemlock. Interesting.

A bright flash of light burst between Sophia and the creature. A powerful wave crashed into Andreas, sending him flying backward. He landed with a hard thump and shifted back to his human form. His head felt like it was spinning, and he tried to make sense of what just happened. As he sat up, a wave of dizziness came over him. His vision blurred, and he held his head in an effort to keep things from tilting in his vision. Groaning, he squeezed his eyes closed and waited for the few breaths it took to calm the spinning.

Opening his eyes again, he saw Ezekiel, Edric, and Sophia sitting and trying to get to their feet. They were tossed near the outside of the cave. The creature, or what was left of it, lay scattered in a smoldering pile of charred bones and ash.

As he stood, he kept his eyes on Sophia who stared at the remnants with a puzzled expression. She shifted her gaze to her hands as she lifted them in front of her. She picked off bits and pieces of black and dropped them to the ground. Andreas realized the gloves she always wore had been destroyed. And the magic that she had done had only burned the creature instead of everything in a fifty-foot radius.

Once he joined his companions and made sure everyone was okay, he set his gaze toward the grove of trees. Something glowing poked its way out from behind a tree. It disappeared only to poke out from behind another one, this time closer. He could tell it was humanoid in shape, but beyond that, nothing. Then it disappeared altogether.

"What is it?" Sophia asked.

He turned to her and smiled at her worried expression. "It's nothing. Just saw something in the jungle." He nodded his head toward that direction.

"Are you sure?" she asked and set her eyes on the same area. "Maybe it's someone who wants to help?"

"After what just happened," Edric said, "whatever it is will likely not come too close."

"Yeah," Ezekiel said, eyeing her with admiration. "You are amazing. Sophia, you've done well to control your power."

"I'm just glad no one is toasted. Well, besides whatever that thing was."

"A manticore," Ezekiel said. "I believe that's what they are called."

"Well, whatever they are, let's make sure we stay as far away from them as possible," Edric said. "Until we get weapons."

Andreas shrugged and settled his eyes on something father in the distance, moving along the horizon. Warning pulsed through his blood. Winston had Tryce curse him with a spell to be hunted by the vexsnare. It was in full effect now and being in the mountain made it easier for such a creature to find him.

"Let's head that way," he said, pointing to the jungle.

Everyone agreed, and they made their way toward the shelter of the trees and grass and whatever else lurked there. Hopefully, that would buy them time to get the curse off him or find a guide to lead them out of the mountain.

CHAPTER FOURTEEN
SOPHIA

This place made the Witch Woods seem like an ordinary wood. The plant life carried a beauty all its own, with its lush foliage and vivid colors. The greens were vibrant and different shades all blended into one. The yellows, reds, and oranges popped with a splendid light. It was like stepping into one of the richest paintings that Nighthelm had to offer, and she couldn't help but reach out and touch a leaf here or a flower petal there. She found herself curious of the land and drawn to it all at once. The magic that surrounded her hummed a lullaby, and she wanted to heed its call.

A mixture of light and color hung in the sky above them as well. Crystals glowed from the sides of the mountain and from the areas where they were scattered across the land, poking up from the ground ever so often, almost like a reminder to their presence. They seemed even brighter when the rays of the setting sun caught them. It was like a whole other world here, and yet she was not too far from Nighthelm.

Creatures, which Sophia could only make a guess at and caught quick glimpses of, quickly faded in and out of sight. The birds made merry chirping sounds but somehow dark at the same time. This place truly fascinated her.

But she couldn't allow herself to be too entranced by the beauty of Ripthorn. She had a job to do, and the last fight still rattled her nerves a bit.

She peeked at her men. Edric still held himself tall and was ever the focused commander, but there was a slight limp to his steps that he tried to hide. And he seemed paler than normal. She knew he wouldn't complain, but he didn't have to. She knew by just looking at him that he was growing weary.

Ezekiel hunched over a bit too much at the shoulders, the color having faded from his cheeks. His eyes seemed a bit sunken in with a dark, purplish shading under them.

Andreas had yet to show any effects. He even seemed a bit stronger.

But of course, none of them would voice their discomfort. It wasn't in them to do so. Two were trained soldiers, and the sorcerer was used to physical drains from magic, she was sure. Still, part of her wondered if they were pushing down their discomforts for her sake.

She frowned. They would need to figure a way out of the mountain sooner rather than later. She wouldn't be able to live with herself if any of them succumbed to the effects of the mountain. Still, she had yet to feel anything from it. If anything, she felt more powerful and even more in control of her magic.

Odd.

Glancing at her bare hands, she wondered if the gloves had the quality of suppressing her magic. Maybe the stunt she had pulled to take out that creature had overwhelmed them and that's what destroyed them. She thought they had a hand in helping her control her magic, but perhaps it was Ripthorn's magic that was responsible? Maybe it made her stronger and gave her more control?

She would have to see herself in action now that the gloves were gone, before she could make an ultimate decision.

"What's on your mind?" Andreas asked, walking alongside her.

"I was thinking about how my magic works here. And what that creature said."

Andreas nodded and seemed to think to himself for a moment. "Those gloves, were they meant to dampen your magic?"

She shrugged. "It's possible, but it's not the first time it was mentioned to me. Back before I met you, I fought off grimms and one had told me I used mountain magic against mountain people."

He glanced at her from the corner of his eyes. The light in them had darkened a bit, which made her frown. He said, "The mystery that surrounds you grows, my love. We'll get to the bottom of just who you are, I'm sure of it."

She nodded. Though it didn't make sense to her. She was a human. At least, that's what she thought. But maybe that's why the oracles spoke to her.

A high-pitched, blood-curdling scream pierced the air. Sophia jumped into action, running toward the direction of the cries as some poor woman continued to scream out.

"Sophia, wait!" Edric called.

But whoever screamed needed help now, not later. She glanced behind her and noted that they ran to keep up with her, albeit a few paces behind.

She broke through the tree line and into a small clearing. A house, sitting inside a lit cavern was where the screams were coming from. Sophia narrowed her eyes on a few thugs raiding the home. They tormented the woman as one held her with a knife to her belly and the others tossed what they could to the ground, scattering clothing, household goods, and anything else as they searched for whatever it was they wanted.

Sophia's magic pulsed just beneath the surface of her skin, and she wanted to summon it when she needed to… not constantly having to restrain it.

"Hey!" she shouted as she rushed toward the bandits. "Let her go and leave!"

Pounding of boots halted just behind her, and she didn't need to look to know who it was. She felt their presence, and that gave her a little more strength.

The bandits turned their attention to her and stopped what they were doing, but they didn't let the woman go. Six more of the thugs come out of the house, holding an older man, as well as another girl and a boy a few years younger than Sophia.

"I said, let them go and leave. Now!" Sophia's voice echoed toward them and the bandits exchanged glances. Some seemed to have muttered things to each other as they gestured toward her and her men and nodded.

They released the people they held captive and turned their attention toward her. One by one, they pulled on their weapons and charged forward.

Sophia was ready. Andreas had shifted to his wraith form and seemed to move much easier. He floated forward and attacked two of the eight thugs. Sophia took on one, disarming him of his sword and taking it as her own before slicing the blade across his neck.

Edric went hand-to-hand with another. Ezekiel

tossed a bolt of light into the fifth. A sixth attacked Sophia and lost a hand before falling to his knees, crying in pain. She quickly ended him as the seventh dodged Andreas's wraith. The eighth...

Where did he go?

Sophia searched the clearing and shadows near the house, but he was nowhere to be seen.

Shit. He got away. Probably to get more of his companions to finish the job.

She turned to check on Ezekiel and Edric. Ezekiel wrapped an arm around his side, hunched over like he was injured. Sophia rushed to him and he shook his head before righting himself.

"I'm fine, Sophia," he said and smiled, though it didn't quite reach his eyes. The dark circles under his eyes deepened and his cheekbones were more pronounced than before.

She knew he was not okay, and only told her he was fine to keep her from worrying.

It didn't work.

She turned and looked at Edric who stood tall but took in exaggerated breaths. She had seen him do so much more in training and barely break a sweat. Though his appearance seemed the same, she knew the fight took a lot more out of him. He nodded at her and she accepted his gesture, just as she had to accept Ezekiel's word that he was fine.

She shifted her gaze to Andreas. He seemed even

stronger than before, which made her suspect the magic affected the both of them in an opposite way than it did Ezekiel and Edric. She smiled at him and cast a second glance to both Edric and Ezekiel before approaching the family the bandits tried to raid. Those thugs failed because of them.

The woman stood with fear alight in her eyes, and her mouth parted as though she was ready to scream again. She had tanned skin, slanted eyes, and skin the color of earth. She took a step back upon Sophia's approach. She sheathed her sword into a belt on her waist and held up her hands to show that she wasn't a threat to them. "It's okay. I only want to know if you can help."

"M-mountainer," she said, voice thick with an accent from a language Sophia didn't know.

It unnerved her that people connected her to the mountain, a place with such dark magic and so much danger. Still, she put that thought to the side and asked, "Can you help us get out of the mountain?"

She looked to the other three as they also backed up. The older male gripped the children at their shoulders and held them close. The boy and girl both kept their eyes on her, widened with fear.

She sighed. These people were afraid of her and her men. She needed to find a way to soothe them. Being closer, the girl looked even younger than she thought before. Her tear stained face still held the innocence of youth. A youth Sophia never got a chance to experience. She looked like the younger version of her mother.

She smiled at the girl and nodded. The girl smiled weakly and gave a nod as well. The boy and man held the same appearance as well. Though with their short hair, she could tell they also had sharp, pointed ears.

She had heard of an earthly race of humanoids that lived down in the mountain. But she never knew what they were called.

"You… fighter from mountain?" the woman asked. Her common tongue was broken, which led Sophia to believe she didn't know much of the language. Just enough to get by, for cases like this one.

Sophia shook her head.

The woman sighed and all the tension that seemed to hold her up left her, and she sank into a bale of hay.

Ezekiel went to the woman's side and laid his hands on her. Light burst from his palms and her eyes widened, but then they returned to normal and she smiled. "Shankoo," she said.

"You're welcome." Ezekiel bowed at the waist then went to tend to the others.

"Can anyone guide us out of the mountain?" Sophia asked.

The woman shook her head. "No. Not know way. All guide gone."

Edric stepped forward. "Where did they go?"

"Lady Naomi," she said with disdain and a nod of her head. As if that wasn't enough, she turned her head and spat at the ground.

"Who is Lady Naomi?" Sophia asked.

"Rules in queen stead. Thug take everything wanted. Leave nothing. Came for daughter." She pointed at the girl.

"Why would they come for your daughter?" Andreas asked. "She can't be more than ten."

The woman nodded. "Slave. All guide locked up in castle. All girl locked up too. They come for son soon." She sighed as her eyes filled with tears. "Be back. They come. Always come."

"Can't you leave?" Sophia asked. "Find a new place to live outside of their control?"

She shook her head. "No. No. Lady Naomi thug everywhere." She gestured with her arms and her eyes grew wide.

Sophia sighed and looked to the family again and did a double take. Ezekiel sat on the stairs to their farmhouse, writing frantically in his book. She shook her head. Even being drained of the very life he had couldn't keep him from writing about new discoveries.

"Blood Queen worse. All war. No sleep."

Sophia shook her head. It wasn't just anarchy in the mountain, but cruel authoritarianism. She may have to visit the castle before everything was said and over with. And it seemed like she had no choice but to find a guide elsewhere. She hated the thought of leaving the family to another group of bandits though. They seemed like good people, just wanting to live their lives as peacefully as possible.

But she didn't want to leave. At least, didn't think they could.

A thought occurred to her. Perhaps they knew of the heirs. It couldn't hurt to ask. They seemed forthcoming with other information. If they didn't know of the heirs themselves, they may have known who to ask.

"Do you know of anyone else from outside of the mountain coming here, when she was a baby?" Sophia asked, pointing to the girl.

The woman looked at her daughter then back to Sophia. Her eyebrows met and she shook her head. "No."

Dead end.

Regardless, she would find out what happened to them. One way or another.

"Thank you for your time," Sophia said and gave a warm smile. "Hopefully, you will have quite some time before the thugs come back. I pray you find a way to seek refuge elsewhere."

The woman smiled and nodded and took Sophia's hand. "Shankoo. Shankoo."

She gave the woman a hug and then turned to face her men. "Let's keep moving."

"No. Stay. Rest," the woman said and nodded to them with a smile as Sophia faced her again. She beckoned for them to follow, and they did, to a small area behind the house, big enough for them to set up camp.

Sophia turned to the woman and smiled. "Thank you."

The woman nodded and returned to the house.

CHAPTER FIFTEEN

EZEKIEL

After receiving bedding, a nice warm meal, and wood for a fire, Ezekiel sat on his makeshift bed reviewing the notes in his book, ruminating on what he had learned so far. He noted that he was weakened since arriving at the mountain, which was to be expected. Honestly, he couldn't believe that they had survived this long since the stories always spoke of the magic being too rich and moved quickly.

He figured Andreas would be fine, considering he was a creature of the mountain. It just made sense that he would live longer than humans. But him and Edric, though... they should have definitely been dead by now.

Musing over the idea as he watched Sophia sleep, he realized it had to be her keeping them alive. Her powerful magic must have had some part in keeping them alive, but he had no idea how much longer that would last, whether it affected her to spend her magic on them, and if there was any reversing the effects.

He used his magic to reach out to her, gently checking that she was okay and not feeling any ill-effects of the mountain magic, but her power hummed in response, stronger than ever. Interesting. This would definitely be something to note in his journals. As encouraging as it was to sense Sophia's strength after being here in the mountain for this long, he knew that he didn't want to test it further and put her or any of the other men at risk.

One thing was for certain—they needed to get out of the mountain, and fast. Before it was too late. Besides, there was a creature stalking Andreas. A monster that lived for the hunt and never stopped hunting once it caught the scent of its prey. The last thing this group needed was a vexsnare arriving at their camp with innocent people present. He had no doubts that was the creature that Andreas saw in the distance. The look on his face had betrayed that much. If only he knew of a way to remove that curse from his newfound brother. They would have one less thing to worry about here in the mountain.

Tryce, the dick that he was, was a force to reckon with, for sure. But that didn't mean Ezekiel didn't have a few tricks up his sleeve that given enough time and preparation, he could use to take him down. Winston along with him.

He watched Sophia sleep for a time and chuckled at the way she snuggled with the sword she stole from the thugs. Damn, he adored his warrior woman. She was stubborn to a frustrating fault, feisty, and full of fire, but she was his. She gave him a family again. Someone to love and cherish beyond himself. He switched his gaze to Andreas and Edric. They were trying to catch some sleep themselves while he had first watch. They were his family too. His brothers. He smiled to himself, appreciating them for all that they did. Each and every single one of them.

He finally had the family he longed for, men he would fight and die for. Things he thought he would never have. And he would be forever grateful to Sophia. Never did he give a moment's thought over whether or not he would die for her, because he would do it in a heartbeat if it ever came to that.

Because of the bond he shared with her and the other two men, sharing her was a small price to pay. Especially when those men were as good-hearted as they come. Especially when those men were Edric and Andreas.

CHAPTER SIXTEEN
EDRIC

*E*dric groaned as he sat up, not feeling well. The magic of the mountain slowly poisoned him, and the effects hadn't gone unnoticed. He was the only one without access to magic, and it seemed like he was the most vulnerable to it. Drained, queasy, he fought back the urge to vomit and forced himself to lie back down. He recalled a time during his training when he and the rest of his barracks had eaten tainted meat and fell ill. He thought then that he would die. What he experienced now made that one event pale in comparison. This was worse. His life was literally being drained. He would exchange this for that moment back in his younger years and appreciate that it would be only temporary.

Sophia appeared in his blurring vision and pressed a wet rag to his forehead.

Ezekiel appeared behind Sophia. "If I can find it nearby, there is a specific type of mushroom that I can turn into a short-acting remedy. It may help to quell the effects of the magic wreaking havoc, for a time."

Edric nodded weakly. Anything to curb the effects of what he was feeling would be a blessing. Sophia smiled at him then looked over her shoulder at Ezekiel. "Please be quick and safe. Take Andreas with you."

"I was already going to begin with," he said. "Can't have Zeke here falling over or something."

Ezekiel groaned and said, "Let's just hurry up and get back. It will take a while for the potion to cure."

"You got it," Andreas said. Both he and Ezekiel turned and walked out of sight.

Edric closed his eyes and focused on Sophia's touch. She was on her knees next to him. He opened his eyes long enough to shift his body and laid his arm over her lap, cupping her waist with his hand. He loved her more than he ever thought was imaginable. Her blond hair was always in a braid of some sort, but this time she had it down and it cascaded around her shoulders like liquid gold. Her beautiful blue eyes were like the sky on a summer's evening and deeper than any ocean. Yet, he could see she was worried for him. He hoped that he would have the strength to help get her through this, even if, in the end, he may not.

Warmth pooled into him.

She gently touched his face, and his eyes shot open. He took in her stare and wondered why his illness was suddenly fading.

It's got to be her.

She smiled, and his lips responded with the same as he pulled her down to him, kissing her with ravish need. Something primal awakened within him, and he needed to give into that need. To be better. To be whole. To be one with her. The animal inside him took over, and his hands moved on their own accord, tearing at their clothing until nothing was left to separate them.

He ran his hands over the length of her torso and back up to cup her breasts. She moaned, and his erection pulsed.

Flipping her to her back, his mouth collided with hers and then he trailed his kisses along the length of her body, pausing at the supple flesh between her thighs. He mouthed the area, flicking the hardened mound with his tongue and eliciting a few gasps and a moan in return.

Gods, this woman…

He growled against her opening before slowly sliding in a couple of fingers, exploring the warm wetness inside her.

"Please," she whispered, and he chuckled, nice and dark. Only for her.

Complying, he rose higher, resting his hands on

her hips as he teased her entry with the tip of his cock. Her blond hair fell loose from its braids and cascaded along the bedding and her shoulders like wheat fresh from the field. Her eyes deepened, and the love and need he wanted to see in them stared back at him.

Emboldened by his newfound health, he pushed the tip of his dick inside her and pulled it back out, repeating the gesture a few times to see the pleasure on her face. Lowering himself to her, he slid completely inside and groaned.

At first, he moved slowly, savoring the delicate, delicious sensation that came from making love to his woman. But the primal need within him took over again, and his thrust became more rushed.

Each touch—each minute he spent with her, made him feel better. Rejuvenated. Back to his old self. And he loved her even more for it. She was his life. Her power and love would help him make it out of the mountain alive.

His orgasm drew nearer as her breaths quickened and her thighs tightened around his waist. At the first sound of her pleasure, his climax reached its height and he released his own pleasure, kissing her as he finished.

Rolling to his side, he pulled her close and stared at the stone ceiling while he caught his breath.

"Guess we found the trick to your health," she said

and giggled against his chest. Her warm breath tickled his skin.

He kissed the top of her head and said, "I guess we did."

Not long after, Ezekiel and Andreas returned. They stopped at the foot of the bedding and crossed their arms.

Andreas said, "If you wanted some alone time, you only had to ask."

"Instead of making us think you were at death's door," Ezekiel added.

"I was," Edric said. "It was Sophia that healed me."

"Uh huh. Sure." Andreas chuckled and shook his head. "At least the trip wasn't an entire waste of time."

Sophia sat up, pulling the fur blanket around her while she fumbled for her shirt. "Why is that?"

Ezekiel said, "We may have found Lady Naomi's castle."

Edric sat up and started pulling on his own clothes. "Then it's close by?"

"Yes. We saw the towers just above the trees. About half a day's worth of travel," Ezekiel said as he and Andreas turned their backs to allow Edric and Sophia privacy to dress.

"Then I think we should go check it out," Sophia said. "We can see if we can track the heirs from there, and maybe we can finally find a guide to help us."

Edric agreed, and now that he felt better after sex, he was eager to get on the move.

CHAPTER SEVENTEEN
SOPHIA

*E*zekiel was right. It didn't take them long to get to the castle, remaining a safe distance away to avoid being detected.

Castle was an underwhelming word for what stood before them. A massive structure with arch-shaped windows reached high toward the stone ceiling, with a tower on each corner. What sky that filtered through openings in the rock above let light cascade over the whitewashed stone that shone blood red.

Sophia wondered if that was why people referred to their ruler as the Blood Queen.

The main gate at the front rose in a high arch on the face of the wall, and black spikes jutted out from the top. Stakes that stuck out from the ground held pieces of broken bodies. They lined the road to the gate, most likely as a warning to those who approached.

A deep chasm flanked the one side of the massive structure, a rock wall flanked the other.

By what she could see, there were hundreds of humanoid creatures forced to labor for the woman, just on the outside of the walls. There was no telling what number was inside. There were a significant number of thugs too, using whips, backhands, and swords to keep the people in line.

One slave in particular didn't even look much older than nine or ten. Her whole body quaked as she worked. But that didn't seem enough for the thug with a whip. He lashed out at her, and the poor girl fell to her knees only to be kicked in the gut and fall to her back. A few others started to collapse, too thin and weak from lack of food and more than likely water. These slaves were treated no better than cattle.

Sophia bit her lip and clenched her fists. These were the people who were ripped away from their homes and families and made into slaves. The injustice toward them really boiled her blood, and she wanted to rush into the fray and free as many as she could before being captured herself. But cooler heads needed to prevail in this delicate situation. The last thing she wanted to do was cause a scene and have the slaves killed off for her actions.

No. She needed to be logical about this.

Ezekiel pointed to a group not within chains. "It's possible we can get one of them to help lead us into the castle. But the likelihood of being betrayed is high."

"Maybe we can offer them something in return," Andreas said. "Barter with them."

"Even trade?" Edric asked.

Andreas shrugged. "Well, as even as we can get."

Edric shook his head. "These people are slaves and likely scared for their lives. No one here will lead us in. We'll have to wait for someone heading this way. A barter could be possible then. But then, what do we have to barter with?"

Ezekiel said, "It will probably be a spell I will have to cast, or a favor Sophia will have to perform."

Sophia shuddered. She didn't like the idea of having to perform a favor. But she had to get her men out of the mountain before they withered away. Sex may have helped Edric, but there was no telling if it would work with the other men, and she didn't think she had it in her to constantly be on her back each time the men grew weak from the magic.

"Whatever it comes down to, we will find a way to make it work. For now, let's make a camp out of sight and come up with a plan in case no one comes this way," Sophia said and twisted on the balls of her feet to step back into the thick of the grove.

∼

SOPHIA

They found a small clearing not far from the path that led them to the castle. While Edric and Andreas checked the perimeter for anyone lurking nearby, Ezekiel gathered some firewood, and Sophia set up the beds and stones for the firepit.

Once settled, they regrouped and had a short discussion of the next step in their plan to finding a way into the castle. Sophia had a feeling that would be where the next clue to getting out of the mountain would be, but she wanted to make a plan on how to first get in. To do that, they needed to do a little recon.

"We could split up," she said. "Take opposite sides and see if there are any secret entrances or maybe find a way to scale the side of the castle and get in that way."

Edric seemed to think about that for a moment. Sophia could tell that the effects of the mountain magic were already starting to reappear in his features. It was almost indiscernible, but the glow of the fire from dinner seemed to bounce right off his skin. Not entirely sinking in or warming the color of his cheeks. "It could work," he said. "But we'd have to be careful."

Andreas said, "Sophia and I can take one side. You and Zeke could take the other."

Sophia nodded. "Yes, and we can meet back here in a couple of hours to share what we have found."

Ezekiel looked up from his furious note-taking and said, "I can cloak myself and Edric so we can go undetected. What are you going to do?"

Sophia said, "I am an expert in stealth, having been trained by Grindel to do such things without being detected. Andreas can use his wraith form if needed."

He seemed satisfied with her response and she felt better having a plan to follow. He nodded. "Sounds like we have a plan. Now, when do we leave?"

"Later, after the guards and slaves go inside," Sophia said. "Until then, we can take turns with the watch. One of us can keep an eye on the castle while the other stands guard over the camp. The other two will sleep, or at least try."

The men nodded, and she sighed with relief. "I'll take first watch."

"I'll take the camp," Zeke said.

"All right," Sophia said. "Edric and Andreas, you get some sleep. We'll wake you in a couple of hours to switch."

With everyone in agreeance, Sophia stood and made her way toward the edge of the camp looking over the castle grounds. She was one step closer to finding the heirs. Everything within her being knew it.

CHAPTER EIGHTEEN
ANDREAS

The chasm to the left of the castle made for an excellent vantage point on an extremely dangerous level. At least that's what Andreas thought as he and Sophia made their way carefully across the steep edge overlooking the canyon below. Edric and Ezekiel took the other side, to see if they could find a secret way into the castle from there.

But they weren't going to knock on the door and ask for entry. Not with the possibility that they would end up on the business end of a pike and hung out to be the next warning on the castle's pathway. Oh no. They were going to *sneak* in and see if they couldn't find out what was really going on behind the wall and maybe get an answer to the location of the heirs.

They made excellent time getting to the castle. Now, the real fun began. Getting in.

The hairs on the back of his neck stood on end. A prickling sensation covered his skin. And a rush of adrenaline coursed through Andreas, and he pushed Sophia into a chasm along the rockface.

"What's wrong?" she asked, her eyebrows knitted together.

But he couldn't respond. He was in full instinct mode.

The vexsnare had found them, and the magic in Andreas's blood boiled with dread.

He pushed Sophia farther into the chasm as the creature drew near, sniffing and shuffling below them.

Sophia gasped and whispered, "It's the vexsnare, isn't it?"

Andreas met her gaze and with a frown, slowly nodded.

She nodded once and they both leaned over to peek at the creature hunting Andreas, both on edge and tense. The horrifying wolf-headed creature walked on all fours. The snakes covering its mane slithered and hissed. The creature's eyes glowed lava red as it sniffed at the rock wall directly below them and mumbled to itself in the common tongue.

That shocked Andreas as he had no idea those creatures could talk. The monsters were mysterious to wraiths, and all he knew was that his kind was a vexsnare's favorite meal.

They watched as another creature that looked

similar to Sophia's yakshi, but more deer-like and not as big or green, approached from around a bend. Sophia clutched Andreas's arm as they watched the vexsnare snort and turn its head in the direction of the unsuspecting prey.

The vexsnare lunged, moving quickly and stealthily. By the time the yakshi look-alike knew what was coming after it, there was nowhere to run. It made a high-pitched, guttural sound as the vexsnare snapped its neck with massive jaws and sharp teeth, pulling out a large chunk of stringy meat. Blood spurted from the wound as the poor creature fell limp on the ground.

Andreas couldn't watch anymore. In mere moments, that would be his fate if he didn't figure out a way to kill that creature.

He couldn't shift. That would draw the vexsnare even faster, making him an easy target. Staying in his human form would make it harder for him to be tracked, but that didn't ease his anxiety. It was worse than what he was originally led to believe. The creature was much larger than the stories told him. The creature was a true force to reckon with, and he would probably need his entire brotherhood to help take it down.

Fighting this creature on the ledge of a cliff wasn't ideal, either.

"Two delicate morsels come my way," the creature mumbled and sniffed around.

Andreas wondered who else's scent this creature could have picked up. He knew he was one, but never considered who the other was.

"We need to regroup," he whispered.

Sophia nodded, and they carefully made their way back to the others, leaving the vexsnare to its meal and whatever other devices that suited it without them being involved.

CHAPTER NINETEEN

SOPHIA

Sophia, lying down, stared at the fire while she thought about the almost run-in with the vexsnare. Everything she had learned about them mentioned how they didn't stop stalking their prey once they caught its scent. They were something of nightmares that weren't supposed to exist outside of fairytales.

But it did. And it was not only hunting Andreas, but something or someone else too. She felt thankful that the creature didn't pick up on them as they stood above it, else they would have likely had a different story to tell about their brush with death and horror.

A shift in the air pulled her attention. She heard something walking at the edge of their camp. She pretended to be asleep since Ezekiel was on watch, though he looked even weaker than before.

She, on the other hand, felt stronger, more capable, and needed less sleep. She waited until an opportune moment and made a move for the woods, under the pretense of relieving her bladder. She snuck through the outskirts of their camp and surprised the person by grabbing her and tossing her to the ground next to Ezekiel.

"What are you doing here?" Sophia said, using the nearby light of the campfire to inspect the girl and make sure she didn't have any weapons.

The girl, beautiful and elvish in features, seemed harmless and frightened as she held her shaking hands up in front of her face, defending herself against a blow that Sophia might make.

"Please don't kill me!" the girl said.

"Then answer my question," Sophia said, backing off a bit to let the poor girl up.

She sat up and scooted closer to the fire, pulling her legs close and wrapping her arms tightly around them. She took in a shuddering breath. When she spoke, she avoided eye contact, preferring to stare at the ground instead. "My name is Torra, I live in a village not too far from here. I'm trying to get out of the mountain and was hoping you would take me with you."

"How do you know we are wanting out of the mountain?" Sophia asked as Edric and Andreas started to stir.

She shrugged. "I've been following you."

"Prove to us you live in a village nearby, then I may consider taking you with us," Sophia said.

The girl nodded and stood.

Edric ran his fingers through his hair and yawned. "What's going on? Who is this?"

Sophia said, "This is Torra. She wants to come with us out of the mountain and is willing to take us to her village that is nearby."

Edric steadied his gaze on her as if there was more beyond what his eyes saw, and she nodded to him once.

Andreas stood and began collecting their things while Ezekiel doused the fire and gathered the supplies they had amassed.

Once they had everything together, Sophia turned to Torra and nodded. "Lead the way."

Torra smiled weakly and turned toward the opposite direction of the castle. It wasn't a long walk, but Sophia could tell that it wore on Ezekiel. They followed the rockface to an opening that led to an oasis with beautiful colored ferns, a clear water hole, and little creatures that resembled sprites, but with butterfly wings and a soft white glow. They danced and fluttered around her and rested on her shoulder as she followed Torra to her village.

Torra walked along a path that was worn into the ground, and through the trees Sophia could see small huts decorating the side of the cliff wall and some even along the ground. Each hut was connected by a series of vine bridges and ladders, as well as branches from the trees surrounding them.

People that looked just like Torra filtered out of their homes and looked to her and her men with distrust. As soon as they took in Torra, their eyes grew with hope and excitement that filled Sophia with joy and relief.

"I have got to get this down," Ezekiel whispered none too softly as he pulled out his book and began jotting down notes like an excited student on the first day of academy.

Sophia stifled a giggle and shook her head. Even exhausted and weakened by the magic poisoning his system, he still found it in him to be excited by new discoveries and writing them down in his book.

Torra stopped at the center of the village where a table full of ripe fruits, vegetables, and a few choice cuts of roasted meats were set. She gestured toward the table and said, "Please, eat your fill. Then we will talk."

Andreas immediately sat down and started pilling a plate with handfuls of each item he looked at. Edric took his own seat and began with smaller amounts. Ezekiel was too wrapped up in his notes to notice the spread. Sophia smiled at the girl before taking her own seat.

"Thank you for such wonderful hospitality," she said.

Torra nodded and was joined by the small number of her people. Andreas and Edric took notice and immediately stood, hands resting over their weapons. Ezekiel finally looked up over the spine of his book with his eyebrows raised and his eyes taking in the situation. The people gasped and took a step back, and Torra's eyes widened. Sophia held a hand up to stop her men and then gestured for them to sit down. "It's okay, guys. They won't harm us."

She knew these people carried a gentle nature just by the way they carried themselves and reminded her of the misunderstood creatures within the Witch Woods.

"Are they the ones we seek, Torra?" A man asked.

Torra nodded. "I believe so. Formidable warriors not from the mountain, though use the magic. At least two of them are."

Sophia's ears perked at that. "What do you mean?" she asked.

Torra waved her off with a gentle smile. "All will be explained wh—"

The man that had just spoken said, "We are in need of warriors like you to free us from the pain and suffering of Lady Naomi's hand."

Sophia gulped. "What do you mean?"

He sighed, shoulders slumped as he said, "We are in

hiding, trying to stay out of the clutches of slavery and suffering of the thugs that work with the woman who leads in the Blood Queen's absence. She is but a mild comparison to the queen, but horrible just the same.

"Many of our people have suffered and died at the behest of Lady Naomi's will. Our children are enslaved and beaten when we don't work hard enough for her. To what purpose, we don't know, but the results are regrettable."

"And those are?" Edric asked.

The man nodded. "Death. Such is the only freedom our people know now, and what we face if we are found."

"You want us to kill this Lady Naomi?" Andreas asked.

Torra nodded. "Yes. Overthrow her and free us."

"What of this Blood Queen?" Ezekiel asked. "Where is she?"

"We don't know," the man said. "But we aren't privileged to such information."

Sophia thought for a moment. This could be their way to get the guide they needed to get out of the mountain, so her men could heal and live. "Say we were to help you. What is in it for us?"

"You seek passage from the mountain, to return to your land?" Torra asked.

Sophia and her men each nodded, said "yes" or hummed the answer.

"Then that is what we will do," the man said. "Will you help us?"

Sophia turned her attention to her men. They each seemed to wait for her to make the decision. But she couldn't guarantee they would make it out alive. She turned to Ezekiel and asked, "How are you faring? Tell me the truth."

He sighed. "Weakened. I should be dead by now, but I'm not, and I haven't figured out why. But we should help these people, Sophia. It's the right thing to do, and we will have guides out of the mountain."

"Not to mention," Andreas said, "fresh new allies."

Edric nodded. "I agree."

Sophia shook her head. "I don't. We need to get you and Zeke out of the mountain before any more damage is done."

"Perhaps," the man said, "our elder arbors could help you. If there is a way to stave off the effects of the mountain, they would know of it."

Sophia's hope grew. "You would do that for us?"

He smiled and nodded.

"Then take us. We will help if they can provide a way to heal Edric and Ezekiel of the effects the mountain magic is taking on them."

"We'll leave at once, then." The man gripped Torra's shoulders and gave an approving smile to her which she returned.

The men quickly finished stuffing their faces

before standing. Sophia shook her head. Regardless of what they faced, they carried a hefty appetite with them.

CHAPTER TWENTY

SOPHIA

Toward the back of the oasis was a cave, isolated, and filled with the rush of a waterfall. Three tree-like creatures were there. They moved freely and were humanoid in shape, with long, limber limbs and sprouts of leaves and twigs that covered the length of their bodies. And for their hair: a collection of leaves and twigs designed differently. They stopped what they were doing to settle their gazes upon Sophia and her group as they entered their private sanctuary.

"Welcome," the woman said, her voice a soft lullaby that drew Sophia closer, marveling at how tall they were, stretching as high as some of the stationary trees within the Witch Woods.

Or, perhaps, it was an illusion of the idea that they were moving, talking, breathing creatures. Regardless, the woman lifted a green finger, tipped with a thorn, and pressed it to Sophia's forehead. The woman closed her eyes and her lids fluttered.

She pulled her finger away and settled her gaze on Sophia. "Interesting, this one."

"Allow me," a tenor voice said, and another elder arbor stepped in front of her. This one was male. He did the same thing and pulled away from her. "Interesting indeed."

"I shall have a look as well," another male's voice said, and he too stepped in front of her and did the same as the two before him.

"A look at what?" Sophia asked, but the elders didn't respond to her.

"Ah, yes. Such a very interesting creature," the second male arbor said.

"Now that we have that out of the way, I need your aid," Sophia said.

"Yes," the woman said. "We know."

"Your connection with your men has carried you all through this journey, while others would have died. But yes, they are weaker," the second male said.

The first male elder arbor approached with two amulets in his hands. He held them out to Sophia. "These will help prolong life, but they will not last forever."

Sophia took the amulets. "Thank you, elders."

The woman approached and held Sophia's chin in

her hand. "You have an incredibly deep magical connection to the mountain, young one. We suspect that connection is far greater than anyone realizes."

"Indeed," the second man said. "You hold secrets even we cannot see."

This was her chance to ask about the heirs. If they could "see" that much about her with just a touch of their fingers, then it was possible they knew much more than that. "And may I ask of the heirs to the Nighthelm throne? Or perhaps how or why I ended up in the mountain?"

The second male inclined his head and turned to his fellow elder arbors. They nodded and he returned his gaze to her. "I'm afraid we don't know much on that. But we do know someone who may be able to help you. For now, aid our friends, and we will send for you once we have contacted him."

Sophia slightly bowed her head and thanked the elders again for their help.

At least it wasn't another dead end.

On their way out, Sophia placed the amulets on both Ezekiel and Edric. They held her close and she kissed them on the cheek. Gently pulling from them, she faced Torra. "A deal is a deal. You've held up your end of the bargain, now it's time for us to hold up ours. We'll take care of this Lady Naomi for you."

Torra smiled and nodded graciously before turning and leading them back to the village.

CHAPTER TWENTY-ONE

SOPHIA

The trek back to the village was quick but gave just enough time for Sophia to mull over the task that lay ahead of her and her men. Once back inside the village, Sophia stopped Torra and asked, "Do you know of a way into the castle undetected?"

She shook her head. "The only way in I know of is through the front gate of the stronghold."

There was a sadness in her eyes that flashed quickly before disappearing. Sophia wanted to ask about that but figured it was likely a family member that was under the control of Lady Naomi's forces. Perhaps Torra had previously tried to find a way in to rescue her loved one and failed, discovering the gate to be the only way in and out of the fortress.

"There is one secret place that overlooks part of the castle. I go there sometimes to…"

She didn't seem inclined to continue, as if the idea caused too much pain. Sophia gently smiled and rested a hand on her shoulder. "Would you take us to this place? It would allow us to scout the grounds and get a better idea of the layout."

She took Sophia in, the girl's big brown eyes were full of hope. Sophia noted a soft glow surrounding the girl's skin. Torra gently smiled and nodded in that meek way she did everything. "Eat first. Then I will take you. You will need your strength."

Sophia nodded and went to the table with her men. She picked at meats and fruits, but she didn't have it in her to really eat. It wasn't that she wasn't hungry. She just lacked an appetite. She found herself wondering if it wasn't partly due to the mountain magic that affected her need for food or if it was her mind being pre-occupied with finding the heirs and putting a stop to Lady Naomi.

As soon as her men had finished eating, she found Torra and let her know that they were ready.

"Follow me," she said and led them through the village and up a set of stone stairs that were hidden behind sheets of ivy that otherwise blended into the rest of the scenery as though nothing was there.

Following a platform was an opening into a stone corridor, lit with beautiful flowers that held a soft purplish-blue glow and was dim but bright enough for them to see where they were walking. It was tall, yet narrow, forcing them to go through in a single-file line.

Sophia loved that the place came with such marvels she had yet to see. It was beautiful and enchanting despite all the dangerous things that lurked in the mountain.

Torra led them through the corridor that inclined toward what seemed like the top of the mountain before leveling off and declining slightly. When they finally reached another opening, it was barely big enough for all of them to stand. The ledge was narrow, making it a precarious lookout point.

But from here, Sophia could see the back side of the castle where a large balcony jutted out from the body of the castle, overlooking another ridge. There was a line of guards or thugs outlining the balcony, standing watch. Torches were lit and placed in such a way to illuminate the area around a woman lounging in the center. She had fiery red hair and copper skin to match. She was dressed only in what appeared to be a very sheer robe. There was a girl standing next to her that resembled Torra, only her skin didn't hold a glow and she was shackled at the neck, wrist, and ankles. The clothing she wore were little more than rags that were torn and stained with dirt and what Sophia knew better than to think as anything but blood.

Torra's hand appeared in Sophia's vision, she held a finger out toward a woman lounging in the center of a balcony. "That's Lady Naomi," she said. "And the girl is my sister."

Sophia's heart wrenched at the pain in the woman's words. She looked to Torra. She nodded once, pressing her lips together as a sheen coated her gaze. Sophia realized then, taking on Naomi was personal for Torra.

"My whole family is enslaved," Torra said. "I only got away because I'm stealthy. That's why Lady Naomi wants me. To use me as a spy." She shook her head and took a shuddering breath. "But I don't want that life. I want to free my family." Her voice cracked at the end and Sophia truly felt badly for her.

"I understand," Sophia said, resting a reassuring hand on Torra's shoulder. Though she had problems of her own, Sophia didn't want to leave the people helping her high and dry. That was just not in her blood or soul. "I will do whatever I can to help you free them."

Torra's eyes widened with hope and she smiled. That glow Sophia swore she saw earlier returned, and her eyes quickly darted to the balcony just before she dashed inside the corridor.

Sophia took a moment longer to study the back end of the castle before turning away and joining Torra.

"Come," she said. "I'll show you the way out of the mountain.

Torra quickly ran into another corridor that Sophia hadn't noticed before.

"What are all of these tunnels for?" Sophia asked.

"Besides discomfort," Edric added.

Sophia ignored the comment. It was uncomfortable for all of them. The space was cramped, for sure. And she figured Edric's size would make the space even smaller.

"Supplies," Torra said. "Before the Blood Queen, we would trade with all the surrounding kingdoms. "But the queen closed all those she could find. Collapsing all known entrances that didn't lead directly from her castle. However, these ones remained."

"Do they not lead out from here?" Ezekiel asked.

"They only view the castle. Watch." Torra led them down a steep decline where the smell of stagnant water and stale air whistled through an opening just ahead of them. She pointed to Sophia and she carefully stepped around the girl to take a glimpse at the opening that was wide enough to give them all a chance to study the cliffside behind the castle. They were about fifty feet up. They didn't have the supplies to climb or rappel down, not to mention there was nothing around for them to leverage their weight with.

But from where they stood, Sophia saw a cave of

sorts that presumably led into the castle itself. But it was barred closed and flooded with water.

"Sewers?" Andreas asked.

"Yes," Torra said. "That is the only way to the exit." She pointed toward a bend in the ravine. "There is your way out. But you can't get there from here. You must go through the castle."

Right. Of course, that would be the thing standing in the way. At least Sophia promised to take care of Naomi. She could do that, find out any information about the heirs, and get her men out of the castle all in one trip.

"Any information we should know of that would help us fight Naomi?" Sophia said, pulling from the view of the sewers and facing Torra again.

"She only fears the Blood Queen."

"And where is she exactly? We've heard her mentioned, just not her whereabouts," Edric said.

Torra held herself. She hesitated to speak. Almost like she wasn't sure how much to say or was fearful of saying too much. Sophia wasn't sure what the case was. As far as she could tell, there was nowhere to hide, but that didn't mean the Blood Queen or Lady Naomi didn't have eyes and ears everywhere.

Finally, Torra took in a shuddering breath and said, "She's scouting for troops to take over the surface. That's why there are so many slaves. Mining ore and rock for weapons. Or learning to fight so they could go to war."

Sophia held the girl. Something told her that even if she were to take out this Naomi and free the slaves, her fight wouldn't end there. It wouldn't stop unless she handled the Blood Queen.

CHAPTER TWENTY-TWO

SOPHIA

The crackling fire popped, sending a spark of ember into the air. The fat dripping from the rabbit Edric caught earlier sizzled into the flames which caused another ember to pop out. Sophia watched the sequence with bliss. The heat of the fire also kissed her skin. Andreas put on a pot of potatoes borrowed from the village. They were all too eager to help. It wounded her heart to know that such cruelty existed within the mountain. The people forced into slavery and worse. Luckily, their fate didn't stop them from helping them out.

Andreas took a seat next to Sophia and poked her in her side. She jumped a bit then narrowed her eyes on Andreas who looked at her with a goofy grin. She giggled and shook her head and shoved him. He played up the act by falling all the way over with a groan. Laughter bubbled out of her, and he joined in with a chuckle of his own.

When their peals of laughter were over, he held her gaze. He was healthy, well, and a light shone in his eyes that wasn't the glow of fire. It was something so much deeper and that made her heart skip a beat and warmth pool between her thighs.

"Get a room," Ezekiel said, trying to force as much disgust into his words as he could, though it didn't work because his smile gave his true demeanor away. He sat on the other side of Sophia, on a toppled over log, writing his notes down.

She was relieved at how much healthier he appeared. The amulet had given him enough health and reversed the effects of the mountain magic. She tried to hide her frown as the elder arbors' words echoed the warning of the amulets not lasting forever. Still, even with the time restriction, she was grateful for the time she could spend with her men, not running or fighting or chasing clues to the heirs.

"Jealous?" Andreas asked, stretching out his legs, crossing them at the ankles and leaning most of his weight on his elbows. All cocky and proud of himself.

Ezekiel sighed as he shook his head and slipped his book back into his satchel and faced Andreas head on. "You wish."

"Both of you can just shove it," Edric said as he

brought a handful of mushrooms and green sprouts of onion to go with the rabbit. "I'm her favorite." He tossed the mushrooms and onion into the pot with the potatoes then faced everyone.

Even he seemed to have been renewed with more energy than he knew what to do with. She smiled at him and watched the banter between the men as they argued over who was Sophia's favorite. She thought about interrupting and telling them none of them were her favorite, that she loved and adored each of them all the same, but the interaction between them proved entertaining. She wanted to hear their reasonings behind why they felt that each of them was her favored choice.

Andreas snorted. "What makes you think you could possibly be her favorite?"

"Because, I am." Edric held his nose in the air and was quite confident by the sound of his voice.

Sophia laughed under breath.

"Actually," Ezekiel said, "I'm her favorite. She chose me for the first date, remember?"

The other two men bickered about the unfair deal and how it should have been them that went first.

Sophia sniffed and shook her head. The male macho scent thickened the air, and she figured she would have to say something before the men tore at each other's throats.

"All of you are my favorites," she said standing up and stretching. "Can we cool our heels now?"

The men gaped at her, blinked a few times, then continued with their playful argument, changing the topic to who was better at the academy. Now that, Sophia couldn't weigh in on. That would just be something they would have to work out on their own.

Once they had finally agreed that because each of them worked for different aspects of the academy, and for Nighthelm itself, they each were best at what they could do—Ezekiel was the best sorcerer. Andreas was the best wraith fighter. And Edric was the best soldier—the dinner was done, and they sat around the fire to eat.

The peacefulness from earlier settled around them again, and Sophia could hear the wildlife in the trees making a symphony of soothing noises. This place was so beautiful and terrifying at the same time. She didn't think it was as bad as the stories portrayed, but the whole slavery thing did reveal some ugly aspects of mountain life. All the more reason to right this wrong and restore what should've been the true beauty of this place.

She took a bite of her rabbit, and juices flowed down her chin. The flavor was herbal and tangy, with the right amount of spice. The potatoes came out crispy and tasted earthy but not overpowering, and the mushrooms added a nice touch along with the onions.

Andreas cleared his plate in no time and pulled out a bottle from within his pack. "I was saving this for when we got out of here, but I figured this was a great time to."

"Where did you get that from?" Edric asked.

"You didn't steal it from those poor people, did you?" Ezekiel asked, a hint of humor in his voice.

Andreas feigned and undignified expression and said, "I'll have you know they gave it to me as a gift for all of us."

Sophia glared at him. "You should have told them no. We already took advantage of their hospitality and they didn't even have to do that."

Andreas shrugged and said, "True, but they refused to let me tell them no. Besides, a night like this could use a little bit of abandon."

Sophia narrowed her eyes on him. She wasn't mad. Quite the opposite. Though she did feel guilty for taking a bottle of their wine from their stores, after being sheltered and fed. She just wanted to make Andreas sweat a little. Out of fun, of course.

"Come on, Sophia. Let's end this night on a high note," Andreas said.

She crossed her arms and frowned, though she couldn't hold it any longer. She burst out in laughter. The men relaxed, the tension easing from their shoulders. Andreas smiled and pulled the cork from the top of the bottle. He took a long pull of the drink then handed it over to Sophia, who did the same and passed it on to Ezekiel, who then passed the bottle to Edric.

The flavor remained on her tongue, which was surprising to her. It was floral, sweet, and rich with a tone of spice she couldn't quite place. Mint possibly, but there was an herby hint to it that paired well with the meal. Her belly warmed with the liquid.

Grindel would have thrown a fit at her for relaxing with such an important mission hanging over her head. She could almost hear the chiding lecture now. She sighed. If only he were here with her. Joining her and her men, with the enjoyment of one evening where they didn't have to be forced to be on high alert. Only relaxing and enjoying one another's company.

She bit back the tears that nipped at her eyes and tried to swallow the lump that suddenly appeared in her throat.

The fact of the matter was, Grindel would've been there if it hadn't been for the Nameless Master. One way or another, she would put a stop to whoever they were and make sure no one else had to lose a loved one because of their actions.

Andreas placed a hand on her shoulder and gave it a reassuring squeeze. Her eyes met his and the smile that he wore. It was gentle. Almost like he knew she was bothered by the thoughts that had just run through her mind. He pulled her close and kissed the top of her head.

She sighed, rejoining the peace of the night for the time that they had. Afterall, it wasn't guaranteed that they would be able to share in such moments again for quite some time.

CHAPTER TWENTY-THREE
SOPHIA

Before the rising sun, Sophia and her men set off to scout the castle again. They stuck to the trees, remaining hidden in the shadows as much as possible. The woods were too quiet for Sophia's peace of mind. Something in the air felt off, and she couldn't quite place what that was.

She looked to Edric. His face was a stern mask of focus. Though, a slight crease rested between his eyebrows and a frown pulled on the corners of his lips. He must have felt the same thing too.

Taking in Andreas, his hands were clenched at his sides and his focus was set on the shadows around them. Even Ezekiel seemed concerned.

Sophia opened her mouth right as an arrow whizzed by her, missing her by mere inches. She pulled on her sword and held it out toward the direction from where the arrow came. But instead of a fight ensuing, a deep, feminine voice called out. "That's far enough."

"Who are you?" Sophia demanded.

"That is not important," the voice said. "What is important is the bounty on your head, Sophia."

So, they knew her name. That made things more interesting.

"What bounty?" she asked, trying to act like she didn't know that there would be one after the stunt she pulled during the trial. She never had the intention of showing her face in Nighthelm until she had the heirs with her, however. To her, the bounty was a frivolous thing.

Edric muttered, "Winston, that prick."

Sophia cast a sideway glance toward him but kept her head forward. She didn't know these people from a pebble on the ground. She wasn't about to let her attention slip or show that she was distracted by any means.

"No. Not Winston. The Nameless Master." The voice chuckled and the bushes just ahead and to the left of them rustled.

Sophia tried to narrow her eyes on the location, but whoever it was that hid within the trees did so with great skill.

"You're rather forthcoming with this information," Edric said. "What exactly does this bounty entail?"

"For you?" the voice responded. "Nothing. You're as good as dead here, regardless. But for Sophia, it means death. Which really doesn't make a difference if you know the details of our bounty, now does it? None of you are going to live long enough to tell the tale."

Andreas growled. "Sounds rather high and mighty of fools who hide from sight."

"We're not hiding," the woman said, sounding a bit irritated. "You have but to open your eyes to see us."

This was getting them nowhere fast. Sophia had better things to do than sit around and wait for these people, whoever they were, to show themselves and attempt to fight her. They were wasting time with all the talk. She needed action, and the magic that burned just below the surface of her skin pulsed with the need to be released.

Sophia said, "Well, if you want that bounty so badly, I suggest you come and get it."

The chuckle that came from the voice encircled them, echoing louder in her head. "With pleasure."

A cat-like humanoid creature leapt from the bushes and went to lash out at Sophia. She swung her blade, forcing the cat creature to lunge back from the deadly slice, then ending in a crouch, tail wagging behind her angrily. She narrowed her eyes on her, and Sophia could only stand there and stare.

The cat creature uttered a growl from her throat and five more of her kind emerged from the trees.

Ezekiel started to mutter under his breath, Andreas shifted into his wraith form, and Edric took a sword (another "gift" from the battle with the thugs) and aimed for the one closest to him.

Sophia's magic sparked along her skin as she held her sword out at the leader of the group. She had never seen a creature like this before, and that also meant she didn't know how to fight them. But damn it all, she would fight with every breath she had.

"What's the matter? Never seen a lynx before?"

Sophia didn't answer. She kept her sword aimed at the creature, ready to kill it to keep herself from dying, especially at the behest of the Nameless Master.

The creature lunged, and Sophia ducked and rolled to the side, narrowly avoiding the razor-sharp claws outstretched toward her. She was sure that not only would it hurt to be flayed by those talons, but they'd leave a nasty scar if she survived. Growls and grunts came from behind her, signaling to her that her men were fighting off the other cat creatures.

She risked a glance behind her to make sure her men were okay. A sigh of relief filtered through her lips as she saw they were holding their own. A weight knocked into her, crushing her to the ground as a sharp stabbing pain punctured her skin. The creature had taken advantage of her distraction and pounced on her.

A purring sound came from her, and she lifted up enough to allow Sophia to breath without the scent of dirt, fur, and the musky scent that cats carried.

"Farewell. Say hello to the gods." The creature lifted a paw into the air and started to bring it down, claws fully extended. Sophia bucked, sending the cat tumbling forward, over her head and to the ground. She quickly twisted and straddled the creature with her sword at the cat creature's neck. The lynx held still, freezing in place.

"Why did the Nameless Master send you after me?" Sophia demanded.

The creature narrowed her eyes on Sophia. She didn't seem inclined to answer, so Sophia let the blade slide just a little along the folds of skin. The lynx made a sound and muttered a word Sophia didn't recognize.

"What?" she asked, angling her ear toward the creature.

"It's a word my people use for mercy," she said, poison coating her words. She seemed loathe to have to ask it of Sophia.

"Speak then," Sophia demanded.

"What the purpose is, I know not. But my freedom was enough to carry out the job."

A pinch formed in Sophia's brow. "What do you mean freedom?"

"Freedom. Free to do as I will without the hindrance of a master. Surely you have been educated in more than just the fighting arts."

"How did the Nameless Master find you?" Sophia asked.

"Does it matter?" the creature asked, sounding pained.

Sophia thought about it for a moment. Ultimately, no, it didn't matter. What mattered was that the Nameless Master knew where she was and sent someone to kill her. A group of assassins, nevertheless. The lynx just wanted freedom, which made Sophia think she was a slave like so many of the people she had come across and had their lives stripped of comfort and the choice to exist on their own terms.

With a sigh, she removed the sword and climbed off the cat-like creature and held her hand out to her. The creature stared at Sophia's hand for a moment then took it, standing up with a nod.

The lynx turned to walk away, then swiveled with her claws out and a roar rushing out of her wide jaws. Sophia instantly plunged the sword into the creature's torso. The roar was cut off as the light from her eyes dimmed and she slumped to the ground in a heap.

Edric, Ezekiel, and Andreas rushed to her, having dispersed of the other creatures. They poked and prodded her for injuries. Aside from the holes the claws left on her chest, she was fine. She didn't even really feel them. It was more of an annoying itch than pain. She shrugged her men off and smiled at each of them.

"We'd better get back before any patrols from the castle come this way. That fight was anything but silent," she said.

"Agreed," Edric said, and Andreas and Ezekiel nodded.

They each turned on their heels and left quickly, sticking to the shadows and listening for signs of being followed.

CHAPTER TWENTY-FOUR

SOPHIA

They made their way back to camp as Torra tore through the woods, eyes widened with fear.

"They found us! They're taking my people right now!"

Sophia ran after her, and Edric, Ezekiel, and Andreas followed behind her. Twigs and branches swatted Sophia's cheeks, stinging with burning pain. She didn't slow down until Torra did, who hunkered behind a boulder and peeked out over the top at a group of Lady Naomi's men who were shackling and beating the village people.

Torra looked at Sophia with tears streaking down her cheeks. "Help them. Please," she whispered.

Sophia nodded and looked to her men, each slightly inclining their heads in affirmation that they were ready. With a heavy sigh, she leapt out of the woods and into the village, sword ready to slice the first throat she came to that didn't belong to one of the villagers.

But the men saw her coming, turning around and smiling viciously, which caused Sophia to stop in her tracks.

What the...?

"Well, well… what do we have here?" an alluring voice asked just as a woman stepped out from behind one of the huts. "Such a beautiful face. An even better addition to my ranks."

It was a trap. The woman was Lady Naomi. She must have known about them snooping around the castle. Sophia bit her bottom lip. She should have seen this coming.

The woman, Lady Naomi, sauntered her way toward them, stopping just outside the reach of Sophia's sword. Naomi studied Sophia with a discriminating eye. Like she was a piece of meat. Sophia stood taller, head held high.

The woman said, "So, you are the one who has been traipsing through the land, killing off my men and trying to rescue these wretched creatures." Her voice was thick like honey, alluring, and very much so matched her appearance. It was like the woman's voice was an enchantment. Sophia almost wanted to fall under it. Except her gut kept her from doing so. That, and the magic that continued to pulse under her skin. She clicked her tongue. "How very naughty of you."

"If you weren't enslaving everyone you could get your hands on, I wouldn't have to set them free in the first place."

She smiled, and damn if it wasn't as bright as the sun and just as warm. This woman had danger written all over her. The voice, her looks, those were all pretenses to confuse and capture prey. Or slaves, in this case.

"My spies spoke the truth about you," Lady Naomi said. "You have incredibly powerful magic." She licked her lips. "Exquisite."

Sophia took a step back and said, "Take one more step and I'll have to cut up that pretty little face of yours."

The woman laughed. She looked around her then back to Sophia. "Feisty too. I'm going to have fun pulling that magic from you. Especially since I know how to use it."

The men shuffled behind Sophia and she was well aware of how badly they wanted to get this fight done and over with. Sophia did too.

"You won't touch me," she said, standing her ground and holding her sword at the ready.

The woman laughed again and seemed unperturbed by Sophia's gesture. "How cute. But I'm afraid you don't have a choice. There are more fighters on my side than yours, and what little work you'll make for my men, it will be worth it in the end. You're about to make me powerful."

Fat chance.

Sophia had heard enough. She would be damned if she let herself be captured and manipulated and have her magic torn from her, much less stand idly by and watch her men be slaughtered with the innocent people of the village.

She didn't think. She only reacted and thrust the sword forward, lunging as she did so. Lady Naomi's eyes widened, and she jumped out of the way.

"Attack now! Keep the girl alive!" the woman called out as she made her way toward the back of the group.

The men clustered in front of them. Sophia slashed and hacked at whoever got in her way. She was going to make sure Naomi paid for her transgressions against innocent people and her threat against herself. Meanwhile, her men, whom she always trusted to fight at her side, took down the thugs that hadn't stood in Sophia's path to the woman.

One by one, men fell before her as she made her way to the woman. When she finally stood before her, the woman smiled. Her hands took on an orange glow and Sophia's magic sparked along her body.

"Impressive," the woman said and shot a beam of fiery light toward her. Sophia dodged out of the way and immediately climbed to her feet and swung her sword, slicing the woman on her upper arm. "Bitch! You'll pay for that."

Sophia lunged out of the way of the next blast of heat and held her hand out as she sent sparks flying toward Lady Naomi's face. The woman ducked, and Sophia wished the woman would stand still long enough for her to be killed. Stepping up her game, the woman pulled a sword of fire out of thin air and slashed at Sophia. She jumped back at the last second, barely missing the tip of the blazing weapon with her torso.

She finally managed to disarm the woman by twisting to the side and cutting the arm that held the magical blade. It dissipated into nothing. Sophia swung her leg out and spun close to the ground, kicking Naomi's feet out from underneath her and hitting the ground hard on her back. The air left her lungs with a grunt, and Sophia wasted no time in climbing on top of the woman with the tip of her blade angled downward.

Sophia went to plunge the blade into the woman's chest as she looked up at her with a strange glint in her eyes. Ignoring the look, she thrust the sword down, stabbing only ground.

Lady Naomi had disappeared into nothing.

Sophia grunted as she pulled herself from the ground, using her sword as leverage. Turning, she took stock of her men. The thugs were all killed and some of the villagers had injuries of their own. Ezekiel limped and fell to his knees.

With a gasp, Sophia ran to him. He had been stabbed. Blood pooled around his fingers. The villagers surrounded her, and two men rushed forward to help him up. The man from before approached them and said, "We know of an enclave that would provide safety and healing assistance to your friend here."

Sophia nodded. "Thank you. Your help is kind. But it's no longer safe for you and your family here. Come with us to the enclave. We can plan for a way to take out Naomi and free the rest of your people."

Torra approached her, eyes frightened and shoulders trembling. "I apologize. I should have been watching for them. I should have done something."

Sophia placed a hand on her shoulder. There was nothing the girl could've done. "It's all right. Can you lead us to the enclave?"

"Yes, I can."

"Good, let's go. I'll still keep my promise to help you and your people."

Though, she hoped she could do so, and get her men out of the mountain before they faded completely. Even now, and with the help of the amulet, Edric and Ezekiel were starting to succumb to the effects of the mountain, growing weaker by the day, though much slower than before.

CHAPTER TWENTY-FIVE
EZEKIEL

The enclave was set half a day's journey from the castle. Though beautiful in its own right, the people inhabiting it were even more enchanting. Races he never heard of huddled together, working for the same purpose. Freedom. Ezekiel wanted nothing more than to pull out his journal and jot down notes on the things he had seen, but his body refused to obey his whim. As it was, the trip took a lot out of him. More than he cared to admit, even though Sophia fussed over him. He liked having her be his nurse. Though he hated that he was in the state he was in. He thought he could be more useful coming up with tinctures and potions to help heal the sick and wounded that filled the enclave more than lying on a comfortable mattress.

When they arrived, the dryads (as he had come to

know them as) spoke of the efforts he and his group had made to help them. As a token of appreciation, they gifted an entire cottage to them. Sophia had insisted that he take the most comfortable bed so he could rest well. He would've rather had Sophia sleep in the bed, but she wouldn't have it. Afterall, he was the one injured and succumbing to the sickness the mountain magic gave him.

"Are you comfortable?" Sophia asked as she checked the bandage on his torso.

"I am." He nodded and smiled at her when she met his gaze.

She was so much more than what she seemed, and the mystery surrounding her was just a fraction of what drew him to her. They had a similar history. A broken childhood. A family stolen from them by death. She had become the center of his universe, and he would never be the same now that she was a part of his life.

"Where's Andreas and Edric?" he asked, hoping for casual conversation.

She smiled. "Playing with the children."

"You're kidding?" His eyes widened. He couldn't quite picture the event.

"I know. I would have a hard time believing it myself if I hadn't seen it with my own eyes." She tucked a strand of blond hair that had fallen out of her braid behind her ear. The motion of that simple thing stirred a fire in Ezekiel's gut.

"Those poor children," he said and chuckled. Stabbing pain shot through him. He winced.

"You should be more concerned with resting," she said, leveling her blue eyes on him. Eyes that threatened to consume him each time he looked into them.

He reached for her hand and wove his fingers through hers. A warm, tingling sensation shot up his arm. She brushed her fingers through his hair. That move of hers pushed him over the edge of all his self-control. He pulled her to him, kissing her with such powerful force. It was like he was starving for her, and she sustained him in such a way no food or drink ever could.

Though injured, just kissing her made him feel so much better. His kisses turned more aggressive and she moaned against his mouth which made his need grow even stronger. Emboldened, he massaged her breasts through her shirt and she responded by climbing carefully on top of him. He worked her out of her shirt while she ran her fingers over his chest, gently scratching her nails against his skin, causing the ache of need to course through him stronger than ever.

If he was doomed to die in the mountain, he wanted to have her one last time. Fill her with his love and be satisfied that he had the chance to be with her once more before his time in this world was over and done for.

Sophia helped him out of his pants and she climbed back on top of him. But he would have none of that. He wanted to be in control, even if it took the last of his strength. But even as that thought crossed his mind, he felt stronger, more powerful. Almost whole again.

She giggled as he tossed her to her back and planted kisses along her stomach toward her breast, where he paused to suck and nibble on them. Her gasp of pleasure and her fingers clutching the back of his head egged him on further. He continued up, leaving a trail of kisses from her chest to her neck and jawline, all the way to her lips.

His cocked rubbed at the supple mound of flesh between her legs and her warm wetness was both enticing and inviting.

He edged the tip of his erection near her entry where her breaths quickened at the mere touch of him. He smiled devilishly at her and kissed her some more. When she least expected it, and her body quaking with need, he pushed himself inside her and damn near exploded right then and there.

Biting back that aching feeling, he focused on the moment, the freeing feeling of being with her like this. The way he felt healed and wondered at the magnificence that was Sophia.

Her love flooded him with so much gratitude. And he was ever so grateful that even if he would die in the mountain, he could never leave her side. She was his family. To live without her would be to live half a life. If even for a day.

As he finished her off, with the echoes of her pleasure ringing in his ears, he himself finished and curled her into his arms as they both worked to catch their breath.

In that moment, he knew he was better. He was stronger, healthier, like the mountain had never poisoned him. She strengthened him and it was through sex with him that he was refueled in both magic and health.

CHAPTER TWENTY-SIX
SOPHIA

Sophia loved the way Ezekiel's arms felt around her and the way that her head was cradled in the bend of his shoulder as he held her close to him. His breathing was slow and even. The color had returned to his skin, and it was as if the magic hadn't poisoned him to begin with.

Sex with her had done the same for Edric. She wondered what it was about her and her magic that sustained the men. Part of her believed it went beyond just sharing a piece of her soul.

Andreas and Edric kept their distance, allowing for her and Ezekiel to have some time together. She loved that they respected her alone time with each of her men. But she couldn't sleep. And she wanted to do something productive with her time like helping some of the people that hosted her and her team.

Pulling herself from the bed, she stifled a giggle as Ezekiel grumbled and tried to keep her close. She succeeded at slipping away from him, pulling the covers tighter around him so he could get more rest. She made her way to the wash basin to clean up before slipping into some clean clothes that had been brought to her from the enclave. Another gift.

Once she was dressed and had pulled on her boots, Ezekiel stirred and sat up on the bed. The blanket fell to his waistline, exposing his muscles. He smiled impishly at her and she blushed with the rush of naughty thoughts that ran through her mind.

"How are you feeling?" she asked, even though she could tell how he much he had improved.

"Better," he said and stretched his arms over his head. He curled a finger at her, beckoning for her to join him. "How about another round of that healing of yours?" His voice was thick with desire.

She smiled and shook her head. "You're incorrigible."

He shrugged and stood from the bed, unabashed, and made his way toward her, pulling her in close, pressing his mouth to hers and making her head spin with heated passion.

A knock rapped at the door. Ezekiel pulled away and went to grab his pants while Sophia answered the door. Edric stood on the other side, flashing a knowing grin.

"Having fun in here?" he asked.

Sophia took in a shuddering sigh and tried not to let her cheeks burn as much as she thought they did. "Fun enough."

"The elder arbors have requested our presence."

Sophia nodded. "We'll be out in just a moment."

She waited until Edric turned and left, then stood before she closed the door and ran her fingers through her hair to comb out the tangles. While Ezekiel dressed, she pulled her hair back into a braid and tied it off with a leather hair lace.

Ezekiel joined her and asked, "Ready?"

She nodded and turned for the door.

They met the elder arbors near an embankment with crisp, clean, blue water not too far from the enclave. The older male stopped them as they approached and said, "Our... friend has arrived, bringing some of the information you seek."

"Excellent," Sophia said with a smile. She went to step past him and was stopped as he held out a branchy arm.

"I highly advise that you check your pockets before and after you speak with him."

She stiffened and looked to her men who appeared just as uncomfortable with that statement. Ezekiel fumbled with his bag and Andreas shoved his hands into his pockets. Sophia wasn't sure what to expect now that the elders seemed inclined to warn them before meeting this friend, and she wasn't so sure the information given would be of use. Still, she ensured everything was in its rightful place before nodding to the elder arbor.

He nodded once in return before turning and walking down a narrow path to where the other two elder arbors were. A strange creature that was hunched over and covered by a hood and cloak stood with them. His back faced them, so she wasn't entirely sure what he looked like beyond that.

Upon their approach, the *friend* seemed to be discussing something at length with the female elder arbor, while the younger male elder arbor stood by seemingly waiting for the conversation to end. He shifted his gaze to them and he stood straighter, eyes brightening with joy.

"Ah, friends, you have arrived well, I hope?" he asked.

Sophia assumed he referred to Edric and Ezekiel and gestured for them to answer.

Edric said, "Thanks to you, we are well."

The younger male elder arbor nodded and clasped his twiggy fingers together. "Wonderful news."

The friend of the elder arbors turned toward them, and Sophia's mouth parted. Things in Ripthorn continued to mystify and amaze her. This creature possessed the features of a weasel but stood on two legs. He looked at the group as they stood in front of him, and he seemed awfully curious about Ezekiel as he approached him and walked around him as though he was a prized trophy.

"Mmm, yes, yes," he said, his voice was tenor but really guttural as well. He then stopped and stuck his nose in the air and sniffed. He turned his head toward Sophia and he smiled, all toothy. "Oh, dear. Even better! I'll take her!" He let out an excited *ooh-hoo-hoo!*

Sophia stood back and gripped the hilt of her sword.

"This," the female elder arbor said, quickly moving toward the creature and putting a hand on his shoulder, "is Rox."

"Rox is the name, making a deal is my thing. Need an enchanted weapon, a rare item? Perhaps a potion that grants you luck and money? Name your price, I'll find it for you." He wiggled free of the elder arbor's grasp and approached Sophia. He sniffed at her and stared into her eyes before shifting his attention to the men and asking, "How much for her?"

Sophia backhanded him. "I'm not for sale."

He rubbed his cheek as his eyes watered. "Fair enough. Fair enough. But if you change your mind, seek me first."

Sophia made a move to slap him again, but he scurried out of range before she could do so. "Listen here, you scurry little rodent, we were told you have information on the heirs of Nighthelm. What do you know?"

"Yes, yes. Information. But such information comes at a price." He stepped a little closer and held his finger and thumb together, rubbing them to insinuate a hefty fee.

"First, I want to know that your information is useful," Sophia said, crossing her arms over her chest. "I'm not paying for useless clues."

"Yes, yes. Young heirs, hid in the mountain, some years back. I know of this." He sniffed the air and added, "Now my fee."

Sophia looked to her men. She wasn't convinced that she should pay for such little help, but her men seemed to give the go-ahead. Edric and Ezekiel nodded, and Andreas gave the sort of shrug that meant "why not?"

"All right," she said, facing Rox. "What is your fee?"

He reached into his pocket and pulled out a crystal vial. "Just a little power." His eyes grew wide and greedy when she took the vial and focused some of her magic into the container. Once completed, she handed him back the vial.

"Satisfied?" she asked.

Rox nodded excitedly. "Yes, yes." He dragged out the last part of the yes.

Creepy little beasty.

"Where are the heirs?" Sophia asked.

He stared at her through one half-closed eye and said, "More answers. More magic." He fumbled through his robes for more empty vials.

"Rox, you have what you need," the older male elder arbor said.

"Yes," the female elder arbor said. "Now is not the time for greed."

Rox eyed the elder arbors from over his shoulder and muttered under his breath. He replaced the remaining empty vials and reached into a pocket and pulled out a key. "This will unlock a hidden door within a mountain cave."

She took the key and settled her gaze on the unusual creature. "Keep talking."

"Stole it off a scary surface dweller that came here a decade ago," he said. "All I know."

"And where is this cave, exactly?" she asked.

Rox's ears perked up and a strange glint entered his eyes. "I'll take you. For a price, of course." He winked at her.

Sophia scoffed.

Edric stepped forward. "You little cretin. You'd better not be suggesting what I think you are."

"You might as well ask to make my sword your bedfellow instead," Andreas added.

Ezekiel said, "Or a curse."

Rox darted his eyes between the three men and then settled them back on Sophia. "All I ask for is a kiss." A few breaths passed and he added, "For good luck and good will."

Sophia narrowed her eyes on him, her eyebrows knitting together. "Why?"

"Because," he said, "even the bravest and strongest of people don't go there. Something dark and nasty fills the place. Curse, methinks. A kiss will protect me."

Sophia wasn't buying it. "Either you live up to your end of the bargain, and take us to the cave, or I'm going to take back that pretty little vial of magic back."

His face contorted over his pointed teeth and he snarled, clutching his robes tighter to him. "No take backs!"

"Then you will take us," she said.

He looked between the four of them again and started to turn around and walk through the elder arbors. But they stepped closer together and blocked his way.

He groaned. "Very well. Fine. I'll take you."

She smiled. *I knew he would see it my way.*

"Let's go. I have other business to attend to." Rox shoved passed them and took the path heading back to the enclave.

CHAPTER TWENTY-SEVEN
SOPHIA

Silent as ghosts, they wound their way through a narrow path that was sandwiched between the base of two mountains. Once they were well past the beginning of the trail, Rox kept his voice low as he told of the sister mountains.

"It is said that everything in life comes in two. This tale is no different. For long ago, there were two goddesses. They were sisters. Twins, in fact. Yes, yes. And they—I think they were sisters. These are them. Sister Mountains."

Sophia stopped listening. The mountain was devoid of any life, and the ground seemed charred in places where other spots looked as red as blood. What plant life grew on the mountain was black and held little beauty compared to the rest of what she had seen of Ripthorn.

There was also a change in the air. Her magic hummed just beneath the surface, waiting to be released. She had a sinking suspicion they were being watched, followed, or both. That vexsnare was still after them, and she didn't want to let her guard down, being distracted with a very confusing tale of how the mountains came to be. Her efforts were best suited to keeping an eye and ear out for any surprises.

Rox muttered something she didn't catch just before he took a sharp left into a crevice within the wall of the mountain that was wide enough for her and Andreas to walk through side-by-side. It narrowed toward the top which made Sophia wonder if it was created with a specific purpose or just happened upon itself naturally through weather and age.

Upon entering, Sophia faced tumbled down rocks, as though something or someone attempted to seal the cave from ever being used or found. Though she wasn't sure what the purpose of that was, she hoped that this place wouldn't end up leading to another dead end or riddle for her to solve.

Rox climbed over the collapsed rock with ease, while she and her men struggled to maneuver through the space without losing balance over the shifting debris. Once they finally made their way over to the other side, Rox reached into his robes and pulled out flint and steel, creating sparks against something along the wall. A bright light burst forth and Sophia noted that there were torches along the walls.

She figured this was the place Rox came to for some of his supplies. He seemed to know the location well despite his resistance to coming. Perhaps something had scared him before. Either way, he pulled the torch from the wall and led them farther into the cave where it was too dark, and the air was too thick and cold.

When they arrived at a spot where the passage narrowed, Rox stopped and handed off the torch to Ezekiel.

"This is where I leave," he said. "I refuse to go further. Not even for another ounce of Sophia's magic."

Sophia agreed that there was something foreboding and unnerving about the place, but not enough to keep her from her goal. She said, "Thanks for your help."

He shrugged as he walked away, muttering something to the effect of "your death, not mine."

Ezekiel passed the torch to Edric and used some of his magic to conjure up some witchlight to go with it. Sophia allowed Edric to take the lead, since he had the torch, and Ezekiel took the rear. This way, if anything was down here, they would know of an attack beforehand. Around them was a maze of natural mineral crystals—stalagmites and stalactites—that led to a door at the back of the cave. All around them gold glittered, and things scurried from the light, deep into the shadows.

As they drew closer to the door, the key began to glow. The aura brightened the closer they got. It seemed to react to some kind of magic on the other side. That brought excitement to Sophia, feeling drawn to whatever lay on the other side of the door. She knew whatever it was, it was an answer. The very moment that door opened, she believed everything would change for her.

Even as they arrived, she noted the door hummed with power. This place wasn't so bad. She couldn't see anything wrong with the cavern other than it being dark and murky. She almost giggled to herself as she inserted the key. The lock clicked, and the door opened into a room filled with massive jewels and treasure and gold.

The men whistled at once and started to search through the items to find the clue they were promised.

Sophia took the back end of the cave, finding a small alcove hidden in the shadows, beyond the jewels. Something glinted in the light as it shifted behind her and she was pulled toward that direction. As she drew closer, she realized it was a coffin made out of crystal. She stepped to the side and looked down at a girl, about sixteen. The coffin pulsed with dim light, slow and steady, reminding her of breaths spaced too far apart or of a heartbeat that pulsed in time to the minute versus the seconds.

The girl was alive. She had to be. That was the purpose of the coffin, it seemed. Sophia wouldn't accept any other reason. This girl was preserved with magic.

Sophia examined the girl's form, finding she was wounded, covered in deep gashes along her torso and arms. It's almost as if the coffin had preserved her in the middle of a fight. Most telling of all was the crest on the pendant around the girl's neck. The royal crest. And that of the royal family of Nighthelm.

"I've found her," Sophia said softly to herself, almost not believing her own eyes for a moment.

She called her men to her, and they came running, stopping short and gaping at the girl in the crystal coffin.

"You don't possibly think…" Ezekiel's voice trailed off and he ran his fingers along the edge of the coffin.

"She's the one," Sophia said. "I feel it."

"Well what do we do now?" Andreas asked.

Sophia said, "Obviously, we need to figure out a way to wake her up. But we also need to find a way to get her out of here."

Edric nodded. "What do you think, Zeke? Finding anything?"

Ezekiel was busy muttering to himself and pulling out his book for notes and such. "I think these are the runes of the druids. Similar to the tablet we found. There's a chance someone who can decipher them is still around here. They may know of a way to get her awake without the wounds killing her."

"You don't think you could do it?" Sophia asked.

He shook his head. "Whoever did this was much more powerful than I am. It would take much more than just me to get the coffin open. Even more to keep her from perishing from her wounds."

"First we have to find a way out of here," Andreas said. "Won't do us much good to resurrect an heir of Nighthelm only to perish within the mountain."

That was true. Albeit, apart from Andreas, her men were starting to show signs of fading again. They were growing weaker, and though she knew they would never admit it, she could tell the trip wore on them and took more energy to get them here than it would otherwise. As she studied the girl in silence, she knew she had a decision to make. Get her men to the surface or stay within the mountain and risk their lives trying to find a way to wake the girl. It wasn't a fair choice, but she knew she wouldn't be able to help restore the heirs if her men were to succumb to the mountain's poisonous magic. Before she did anything for the girl, she needed to know exactly what she was dealing with, who she was, and who had the power to wake her and heal her. Not to mention what befell her and caused her to be placed in this coffin.

"He's right," Sophia finally said. "We'll have to come back when we can. Then we can wake her and find out if she's an heir."

"It's possible she is," Edric said. "Few ever met the heirs in person and even fewer know what they would look like. Though we always suspected the heirs to be men."

"Maybe that was part of the point of keeping them hidden," Andreas said.

"Either way, we will have to come back. We can't do her any good now," Sophia said. She stared at the girl a little longer, something pulling at the back of her mind. There was more to this girl than met the eye. "Let's not share what we've found here until we know for sure who she is and why she's here."

The men agreed, and they turned around to head back to the enclave.

Sophia couldn't help but ponder the mystery of the girl in the crystal coffin. She finally had a lead. A promising one. She felt even closer to finding the heirs, and she had a feeling she was either an heir or was associated with them. First thing was first, get her men out of the mountain and fast. She didn't think they could survive in the mountain much longer. There was only so much her magic could do, and the amulets did well at staving off the effects, but like the elder arbors said, it wasn't a permanent fix and could only work for so long.

Her new mission: to get her and her men out of the mountain before they died and to return once they were fully prepared to bring this girl back from her crystal-encased death.

CHAPTER TWENTY-EIGHT
ANDREAS

After they returned to the enclave, Sophia was chomping at the bit to leave. She insisted on a plan of attack so that they could get out of the mountain and return as soon as they were prepared to take care of the girl in the crystal coffin. Something else bothered her, and he had a feeling it was the ever-declining health of Edric and Ezekiel. Andreas knew she blamed herself for it, and he was sure she wouldn't hear of it otherwise. Instead, he offered to go on a scout to find a way into the castle.

Torra almost begged to join him. He figured she still felt guilty with how things went down when they first came across Lady Naomi, but he insisted he would work quicker on his own. She nodded and said, "There are a few ways to get into the castle. You might find the side closest to the mountain worth pursuing."

"Anything more specific?" he asked.

She shook her head. "You'll know it when you see it. There's a boulder."

Following the directions Torra gave, he went to the side that faced the mountain. There was enough of a space to walk through and archer windows lined the top wall of the castle. He found the boulder she referred to, but nothing that hinted at a way inside. Looking around and finding he was alone, he shifted to his wraith form. He felt weighted down still but was able to fly to the top of the wall and peek into the archer window. He was shocked to find it empty. Lady Naomi must have grown cocky in her power to leave her vulnerable areas unguarded throughout the castle. But there could be traps in place of guards.

From this view, he caught sight of the boulder and saw that there was an iron grate behind it. He floated back to the ground and shifted back into his human form. Returning to the boulder, he found that it was movable. The grate hung on hinges and seemed to lead into the belly of the castle.

"So that's what she meant?" he asked himself.

Since they needed a way to get to the sewers, this was the best option they had.

Satisfied, he started on his way back, and then he sensed the vexsnare near again. He kicked himself for using his wraith form, knowing the creature would be able to track him much easier, but he also needed a way into the castle, and that was the only way he had access to it that would accomplish the goal.

Man, they needed to hurry up and get the hell out of there. Hiding in the bushes, and controlling his breathing so that he wasn't detected, the vexsnare prowled not too far from him, sniffing around and muttering to himself.

"Finish dinner from thirteen years ago…"

Finish?

A pinch formed in the center of his forehead at that one. Something didn't seem right. He thought the vexsnare had been after him all this time. Sure, it mentioned someone else the last time he came uncomfortably close to him and Sophia, but it hadn't made much sense.

"Ah, little Sophia… all grown up and delicious. Come to finish what we began…"

Foreboding settled in his gut. Those words held a haunting history. If it was Sophia that he was after as well, then that meant that they were bound to cross the creature sooner rather than later. And there would be no escape without a fight.

But more than that was his knowledge of Sophia's past clicking into place and making more sense. She was found in the mountain. And it took massive trauma and agony to break someone's soul. If this was the creature that had come after her all those years ago, it was possible that it wasn't able to finish the job and what the creature had done was enough to break her.

That had to be it. It made too much sense for it to be otherwise.

He struggled with the decision on whether or not to tell her. He was overcome with the need to protect her and didn't know enough about contritums to feel comfortable to tell her. He didn't want to shatter what was left of the soul she had and undo all the progress she had made.

For now, he would keep his realization to himself. At least, until he knew without a doubt, telling her wouldn't irreparably damage her.

Keeping as far away from the vexsnare as he could, he continued on his way back to his woman. Though he wished he could return to his wraith form, he knew the vexsnare would hone in on him. He missed being able to use his form and the power it gave him, but he couldn't risk shifting again while so close to the vexsnare. A move like that would lead it directly to the enclave and put everyone at risk. Especially Sophia, and the two men he had come to know as brothers.

CHAPTER TWENTY-NINE
SOPHIA

Sophia had busied herself with gathering weapons and rations. While she worked, she reminisced on the findings and everything she had learned about the heirs. Her motivation to leave the mountain pushed her. She had to save her men, and the girl, but to do that, they had to leave the mountain. To leave the mountain, they had to go through Lady Naomi's castle. That would likely result in a fight, so being prepared meant also accounting for the possible outcomes.

"Sophia," a soothing voice said. She instantly recognized it as the female elder arbor.

Sophia turned and faced her. "Yes?"

The female smiled and said, "Torra's guilt weighs on her. She blames herself for what happened back at the village."

Sophia nodded. "I've already forgiven her." She added a smile so that she could end the conversation and get on with preparing for a fight and leaving the mountain.

"Might you do her the honor of allowing her to guide you to the castle?" the female elder arbor asked. "She wishes to make up for the misunderstanding and warns there are endless tunnels and labyrinths within the castle that ends in steep drops. It would give her peace of mind to see you safely through."

"There's no need," Sophia said, and her eyes caught sight of Torra standing off to the side, appearing forlorn and possibly abandoned. She supposed that forgiveness wasn't enough. She sighed. "On second thought, she can guide us. That would be very helpful."

The female elder arbor smiled. "Excellent. She will be pleased."

"My pleasure," Sophia said.

The elder arbor turned and returned to Torra. The girl's face lit up as did that strange glow. Sophia smiled. At least she was happy.

Sophia finalized the last of the preparations as Andreas returned from his scouting. He shared with her the information he found out about the entrances not being guarded. She thought that was odd but shrugged it off, believing his explanation that Lady Naomi had grown cocky.

Once Edric, Ezekiel, and Torra joined them, they set off.

The trip to the castle was uneventful, and Torra led them to a secret entrance hidden by a hollow boulder at the front of the castle.

Torra seemed nervous. "Watch your footing. The way is dangerous."

Concern rippled through Sophia, setting her intuition on high alert. She shrugged it off, though, as the girl met her gaze and she smiled in that gentle way she usually did. Torra always gave off the impression that she was opposed to conflict. Maybe she wasn't used to war and the possibility of death.

Once on the platform at the bottom of the stairs, they climbed down from the grate. Torra led them down a steep, dark tunnel. Ezekiel conjured a few balls of witchlight to walk by, making it easier to see where they were going. When it eventually evened out, a doorway opened into an abandoned chamber under the castle. It was dark, the shadows too thick to see through, though it is evident that a ledge with windows hovered near the ceiling. Torches hung on pillars that bordered the room, and there were small statues of creatures Sophia could only hint at standing on podiums between the pillars.

Torra ran to the center of the room and yelled, "I've brought them!"

What? Sophia couldn't believe her ears or her eyes.

That sweet, elvish, gentle girl who was meek and shied away from conflict had just betrayed her to the one person she asked Sophia to kill. She thought she could depend on the girl to help lead them out of the mountain. But the girl gave them over to Lady Naomi and her forces. That stung. Sophia's trust in the girl was forever broken. That pain quickly turned to anger.

The torches instantly burned to life, illuminating the shadows as hundreds of soldiers crawled out of every possible hiding spot provided in the room. Sophia and her team sprung for a fight. She narrowed her gaze on Torra. She would be the first to die for betraying them. She had shown her enough mercy, and now the traitor needed to die.

Just as soon as Sophia made a move toward the girl, she was overwhelmed by a group of soldiers. They pinned her down before she could so much as pull her sword or conjure her magic to disarm them. Magical cuffs were slapped onto her wrists to prevent her from using her power. Or, at least they limited her abilities as she still felt her magic humming beneath the surface of her skin. She just couldn't bring it forth.

Sophia's eyes found Torra's again, and though she seemed apologetic at first, she lifted her chin defiantly and said, "I demand that Lady Naomi lives up to her end of the deal."

"Very well," the woman said. "Your people are free to go."

Satisfied, and with tears in her eyes, Torra said to Sophia, "I'm truly sorry. I did it for my people. The elder arbors may never forgive my betrayal of their savior, but it was a small price to pay for the freedom of my people. The people that I love."

Sophia cried out in frustration as she was dragged into the shadows. Away from her men and away from the girl that betrayed her. She wanted blood, she wanted to fight. She wanted a way out of the mountain, so she could see her men live. All of that was taken from her, and she would be damned if she didn't go down without a fight.

CHAPTER THIRTY

SOPHIA

The shackles felt too familiar. They were similar to the machine's magic. The one that pushed her to her limits during the Headmistress's tests.

Lady Naomi led her men and Sophia into a tall room with a domed ceiling that let daylight stream in from overhead. And it struck her as a way out of the mountain. That would make sense. The castle would need a few exits out of the mountain, and it was extremely plausible that the entire fortress was an elaborate gate barring the exit from the mountain.

She considered Torra had lied to them from the start. Though some of her actions didn't seem as so in hindsight.

The thugs tossed her into an elaborate machine

made of crystal and metal, and she clenched her teeth as she was strapped in.

Lady Naomi walked casually through the room, eyeing her. She seemed rather at ease with the progress of the events that landed Sophia in this predicament.

Sophia wanted to wipe that proud smirk off her face and said, "Interesting to bring me to a room with my exit. I think I'll be going now."

The woman laughed. "Oh, I doubt that."

"Why? Because I'm strapped to this machine? Please. Simple. And when I do get out, you'll have nowhere to escape except for going up."

"If you are working to pry out of me that this," she pointed up, "is the only exit out of the mountain, then you would be correct. Which makes this all the more pleasing. Watching you stripped of your power when so close to your goal. That was your goal wasn't it?" She faced Sophia with her hands behind her back. "To leave the mountain?"

Sophia didn't answer. Instead she jutted her chin forward and braced herself for what would be another painful experiment.

"This is my gem and testament to the power I've accumulated for myself." She pulled a key dangling on a chain from between her breasts. "This is the key to the only way out." She tucked the key back into place.

"You, however, won't be leaving this place. In fact, you'll never see the surface again."

Sophia watched as the woman approached the switch on the outside of the door into the machine. She flipped it on, instantly searing Sophia's nerves with the electrifying pain that threatened to burn her from the inside out.

Through the pain, Sophia gritted her teeth and watched as crystals filled with her magical power, glow when full.

Lady Naomi smiled and said, "Do you like my contraptions? The idea of these crystals is to store your power for later use. I'm going to slowly bleed you dry, Sophia. You and your men."

She snapped her fingers and curtains opened to reveal her men, each in similar machines and also being drained.

Anger blossomed in Sophia's gut. She needed to save her men but breaking from the machine was going to take time and effort. Straining against the machine, she asked, "Is this what happened to the heirs of Nighthelm?"

Lady Naomi's expression twisted into genuine confusion. "Who?"

Dammit. So, the heirs weren't in the castle after all. Another dead end. Not that she didn't have high hopes that the girl in the coffin was an heir. She just needed to know if they were here, in case she wasn't one.

But the question worked to gain a bit of a distraction. She looked at her tattoo. She felt Haris deep within her soul, itching to come out. She had never tried to call on him without touching his image before, but this time, she desperately needed him. Biting against the pain, she focused herself and uttered, "*Vocavi.*"

Haris's form disappeared from Sophia's arm, and green smoke appeared behind Naomi. He solidified right behind her. He must have known about the danger and wanted to appear right where he knew she would need him. He speared Naomi with an antler, knocking her off balance and taking the key.

That's my yakshi.

But the woman regained her composure and stood, turned, and started to blast Haris with fire magic. Being an earth creature, he didn't stand much of a chance. Sophia needed a way out of the machine and fast.

Funneling all her magic into the machine, much like she did before, the contraption made grinding and metallic screeching noises as crystal started to shatter.

Lady Naomi looked over her shoulder at Sophia and glared. She increased the fire toward Haris, and he luckily was able to hold her off. But for how much longer, Sophia wasn't sure.

She focused on her magic, summoning it, calling it to the machine. Sparks covered her body and pulse with intense pressure. A kick in her gut made her question if anything would be left once everything was said and done, but she couldn't stop it now. She could only try to control it by focusing her energy on the machine and not everything in the room.

Her bones felt like they were being crushed under a great weight, and fire burned through her veins. All at once, the energy blew, knocking out the machine and freeing her from the seat.

She didn't incinerate everything within a fifty-foot radius around her. She didn't pass out, and she wasn't naked, for once. She stood tall, feeling more powerful than ever. The change in her suited her. Power fit her like a glove. And now that she had access to the key, she could free her men and leave this place for good. But she was a woman of her word.

Despite Torra's betrayal, she would still live up to her end of the bargain and end Naomi once and for all.

CHAPTER THIRTY-ONE

SOPHIA

Sophia's gaze met Lady Naomi's. Fire burned within the woman's eyes as Sophia held her head high and made her way toward her men. Haris knocked his antlers against Naomi, deflecting a bolt of fire she shot at Sophia. He pinned her against the wall to allow Sophia to work.

She freed her men while alarms echoed throughout the fortress, threatening to rupture her eardrums. After flipping the switches on the machines and helping each of her men to stand—they didn't look like they were doing too well—Sophia turned to find hundreds of guards pooling into the room they were in.

Sophia's eyes darted to Haris, she called out to him, "Find the exit."

He huffed, shaking his head.

"Haris, you're our only hope. Please, find it. We'll be fine here." She pushed as much love and warning into her words as possible. "We will need to escape, and quickly."

His eyes focused on hers, filled with pleading to let him stay and fight by her side. But she couldn't let him. She knew he would die if he stayed, and she had to find the exit so they could all escape. She shook her head once. He finally ran off in a rush.

Sophia turned and faced Lady Naomi, who seemed out of breath, and rage burned in her eyes the color of magma. She smiled wickedly at her and took steps backward to try and escape the room or hide behind her thugs.

She wanted to run after the woman, but her men weren't recovered from the machine. She couldn't leave them to their deaths.

"Go," Edric said. "We'll cover you."

She met his gaze, then Ezekiel's and Andreas's. Each of the men gave a nod and prepared to fight off the guards. Worry for her men filled her. She dreaded leaving them, but she had to fight Lady Naomi and end her one way or another.

Sophia dashed toward the wall, letting the last of the guards file into the room. She watched as Edric and Andreas started to fight them off. The two men took weapons from them, quickly killing them, while Ezekiel used his magic to disarm the others.

Taking in a deep breath, she scurried along the wall to the back of the room where Lady Naomi leaned against the wall, nursing her wounds from Haris. She panted as she tore at her clothes to mend puncture wounds in her arms.

She kept to the shadows as she moved closer, she pulled a sword from the thug closest to her. He had two, so it wasn't like he needed both. Her magic hummed along the surface of her skin, sparking and arching. Once she was close enough, she stepped into Naomi's view. The other woman's eyes widened, and she searched for a way out. Realizing there was none, she stood straighter and rolled her shoulders.

"Come to finish the job?" she asked, voice soothing and dangerous.

"I have," Sophia said and held the sword out toward her. Her magic sparked along the blade as well. She wanted to marvel at that and see what else she could do, but Lady Naomi pulled her attention.

"Such a shame we met under such circumstances. We could've been friends." Her eyes glowed with the fury within her magic and Sophia noted, on the edge of her vision, Lady Naomi's hands started to glow with fire.

"Too bad I would never be friends with you." Sophia jutted her sword closer to the woman who just smiled and shook her head.

"Silly little girl, you would be under my control.

Just like everyone here. Your will would be *my* will. And there would be nothing you could do about it."

"Is that how you enslaved all the people of Ripthorn?" Sophia asked.

She smiled. "I do have a way of making people do what I want them to. That's the beauty of all of this." She gestured around her. "I serve my queen beautifully, don't you think?"

No. "You've forced people under your rule. Made a majority of them your slaves and killed anyone that stands against you or threatens your seat." Sophia shook her head. "You're a tyrant who will not live to see another day."

She chuckled, long and dark. "We shall see about that."

Naomi conjured her fire sword, the flames turned blue and white. She admired her work for a moment and shifted her gaze to Sophia, who narrowed her eyes on the woman and summoned all the strength she had within her. Her sword hummed with the electric static covering her blade. She swung at the woman, and her attack was parried with a swing of the woman's sword.

Every step Sophia made, Naomi anticipated and parried with an attack of her own. Though Sophia managed to avoid being burned by the sword, her skin still blistered with the heat of the narrow misses.

Anger boiled through her veins and she pushed more force, more magic, into her attacks.

Lady Naomi's eyes widened, and she was forced back a few steps with each strike, but she still managed to block and parry the blows. Sophia knew she wouldn't be able to keep up the intensity forever. She had to think of a way to disarm the woman. But Sophia's gaze was captured by a glint on the woman's forehead. Sweat. She must have been stepping up her game to try to best Sophia. If she could out-maneuver the woman and maintain her intensity, she could kill the woman before she drained Sophia of her energy completely.

"What's the matter, *girl*?" Lady Naomi asked. "Running out of steam?"

Sophia ignored the woman's comment as well as the way she emphasized "girl." She was more concerned with checking on her men. Ezekiel was still pale, but he managed to hold his own. Edric, ever the soldier, refused to let his weariness show even though she knew that he too was weakened by the mountain magic.

Lady Naomi tried to take advantage of her distraction and attacked. Sophia saw it coming, and parried, reciprocating the attack. She looked to her men again.

Andreas fared quite differently. He fought in his human form, even though he was stronger and faster, and much, much deadlier in his wraith form. Still, he fought brilliantly against the thugs, managing to take them down. But his shoulders were tense, his arms shook, and sweat soaked his hair, making it stick to his forehead. If he shifted, he could take the majority of these assholes out within a matter of minutes, but she knew the vexsnare was after him. And his wraith form made it so much easier to track him.

She knew the creature had been close by, narrowing in on her man bit by precious bit. And seeing him strain against the urge to shift made her wish he could change. But the last thing they needed was the vexsnare on top of the army of thugs and Lady Naomi.

She dodged a fire ball, ducking and rolling to the side then shooting out a bolt of light toward the woman. Naomi didn't have time to block. The bolt smashed into her chest. Jumping up, she stood over the woman with her feet on either side and held her sword aimed at her chest.

Naomi gasped and clawed at the charred circle in her chest as her eyes darted around for what Sophia assumed was a means of escape.

Not this time.

The woman's eyes met Sophia's, and the realization that she was going to die filled them. Sophia didn't particularly enjoy seeing that in the woman who had come to acknowledge her fate. But it was a necessary means to an end.

Sophia said, "The people of Ripthorn deserve a life outside of chains and fearmongering. They deserve freedom of will and the chance to prosper on their own terms. They deserve a life without you."

She shoved the sword downward into the woman's gut. Lady Naomi's eyes widened as she grasped at the blade in futility. As the fiery light faded from the woman's eyes, her skin started to ash and flake.

Taking a few steps away, Sophia watched as the woman's body seemed to catch fire and burn away into nothing.

Her end of the bargain had been satisfied. But the fight wasn't over. She turned and started to fight off the remaining thugs with her men.

CHAPTER THIRTY-TWO

ANDREAS

*E*ven in their weakened state, Edric and Zeke fought admirably. He was proud to call them brothers and even grateful that they fought at his side. Though, it pained him to fight in his human form. It seemed to drain him of his energy faster, and he couldn't move as quickly as he wanted or fight as hard as he needed to.

Despite all that, he wouldn't have chosen any other men to fight alongside him. They complimented each other. Ezekiel with his wit and magic. Edric with his strength and tactics.

The thugs attacked at random. Some of them seemed too inexperienced, with fear in their eyes and their skin paling. They would be the ones to watch out for.

A thug approached, swinging his sword toward

Andreas's neck while he jabbed at another. A rush of heat burned past him, blasting away the thug who had swung at him, and he glanced over his shoulder at Ezekiel who nodded.

Andreas smirked and nodded in return.

Look at that, the sorcerer saved my ass.

That's when Andreas caught the sight of a thug moving in the shadows, inching up behind Ezekiel. Andreas threw his sword. Ezekiel's eyes grew wide, his mouth agape. Andreas wasn't worried, the sorcerer was smarter than to step into the path of the blade.

It landed true, in the gut of the thug.

Ezekiel stared at the thug for a moment then pulled the sword out and tossed it back to Andreas. All the while a look of confusion and relief covered his features. *Yes, Zeke, the wraith just saved your ass.*

Though Andreas tried to ignore the paled expressions and slightly more sluggish movements of his two brothers, he knew the fight would drain them to a devastating point. He feared what lay beyond the room for them on the way out and just how long it would take for them to recoup from the mountain's poison.

Stepping up his game, he fought harder, faster, burning through every ounce of energy within him, all the while fighting his urge to shift into the wraith that kept calling to him. Pleading with him.

He frowned. The wraith was near death. He was

near death. Andreas knew that if he didn't shift, he would die. But if he shifted, the vexsnare which followed him throughout their journey through the mountain would find him. And there was no way he could face that creature in the state he was in. Shifting would mean death as well.

For the time being, he would have to trust in his brothers and fight with everything he had until his final breath and heartbeat.

He searched for Sophia, to see how she was faring and found her at the back of the room, fighting thugs, slowly making her way toward him, Edric, and Ezekiel. His heart skipped a beat at the sight of her focused determination as she took down each man on her own.

She certainly did better than he and his brothers. And that didn't really surprise him. She seemed to have grown much stronger compared to when she was outside of Ripthorn. He wanted to analyze that more with his brothers and her, but that would have to wait for a time when they weren't in the mountain and his brothers slowly dying from the poisoning effects of the mountain magic.

A sharp, stabbing pain shot through his back, radiating throughout his torso. His knees gave out from under him, sending him to the floor with a thud. Edric rushed toward him and leapt over Andreas, into the thug that stabbed him in the back.

Sophia rushed to him. Ezekiel used his magic to collapse the entry, preventing any more thugs from entering the room. He approached and also knelt by Andreas's side.

"That was the last of my magic," he said. His face was sunken in. Like he had lost too much weight. The magic was close to taking his life. "But that should buy us some time."

"I have to shift," Andreas said. "Or I'm as good as dead."

He knew the weight of his words and that it would mean the vexsnare would zero in on him quicker. But he had no choice. The wound he endured was taking the last of his strength.

Sophia's brow creased with worry, but she nodded. "Do it."

He shifted. He instantly sensed the vexsnare pinpoint him. It had finally found them.

Though he felt the joy of being in his wraith form, his desire and need to protect his family overwhelmed everything. He needed to defend his family from the creature that loved the taste of wraiths, but he knew if he fell, so would Sophia, Edric, and Ezekiel.

Resolved, he floated farther into the room. Haris rushed in.

Sophia asked, "Did you find the exit, my friend?"

Haris nodded his big, antler-covered head, trilled, and stomped his foot. Andreas wondered if he too could feel the dangerous creature heading toward them.

"Let's get out of here," Sophia said.

"Finally," Edric said. A small bit of the tension in his shoulders eased.

"Lead the way, Haris," Ezekiel said.

They all filed out of the room, following Haris to the exit. All the while, Andreas was stuck on high alert, hoping beyond all hope that they could either out-run the vexsnare or fight it off.

CHAPTER THIRTY-THREE

SOPHIA

Sophia knew deep in her gut that the fight was long from over. She and her men followed Haris through twisted and turning tunnels. They ran, urged by the danger hounding them, nipping at their heels. The vexsnare. She hoped that any remaining thugs loyal to Naomi would hold off the creature long enough to allow her and her men to get out of there.

Andreas took the rear, though she wished he would allow her to take that position. She narrowed her eyes on him and said, "If you dare sacrifice yourself for us, I will *never* forgive you."

His red eyes blinked at her as he continued to move. She shook her head, biting her lip against her worry that the vexsnare would overtake them and snatch Andreas from her before she was aware the creature was even there.

If she entertained that thought much longer, it would force her to take the rear instead, but thankfully they arrived at the gate. She pulled out the key she took from Lady Naomi and unlocked it with a satisfying clink. Pushing the gate open, everyone filed through and she could see sunlight up ahead.

As she drew near, her mind became focused on fighting Winston and drawing up part two of their plan. But something hazy covered her, creating an odd sensation. Her world tilted and started to spin. Black mist rolled across the ground as her vision blurred.

She could hear the men. Each of them called her name, but she couldn't find them. Their voices seemed too far off. Almost like a memory. The feeling that overcame her was coupled with a strange sense of familiarity.

Another voice called her name. A female's this time.

Images cropped up around her. She was within a tunnel, like the one she had just stepped into. But in this tunnel, she was younger, and a girl was with her. However, the other girl's image was blurred too much to see clearly.

"Sophia, run! Get out of here!" the girl said.

Sophia's younger self cowered into a crevice by a large rock.

Their means of escape was blocked. And there was no going back the way they came. The girl with her, the one who told her to run, started to back up as a large, terrifying creature cornered them.

The girl looked to Sophia and uttered a word that didn't make sense to her young ears. The large rock shifted, and the sound of grinding stone pierced her ears as the rock sealed her in the crevice.

Sophia sucked in deep breaths of musty earth and mineral dust as the screams from the girl tore into her spirit like nothing ever had. She peeked through a small crack and saw the beast drive its claws into the girl she knew and loved but couldn't remember.

The girl fell, and Sophia's soul was broken as she screamed and cried, tearing her nails down to the tips of her fingers trying to claw her way out of the opening, so she could hold the girl and will her to life.

But it was no use. The uncontrolled magic within Sophia's blood bubbled to the surface, threatening to lose control.

She was different now. She was in control of the episode that threatened to level a fifty-foot radius around her, wiping out everything but her. Sophia controlled the magic though. She's more powerful and capable than ever before. She tamped down on the magic rolling beneath her skin.

Disembodied words echoed through her mind, encasing her with the knowledge she had long forgotten and had tucked away with the horrifying event that broke her soul.

"She will overthrow the crown and raid Ripthorn for a Nighthelm master. Teach her to control her magic, and you will be well rewarded..."

"It shall be done. What of the duchess, Master?" That sounded a lot like Mistress Mittle.

"I'll see to her..."

That voice was too familiar, but Sophia couldn't place it. It was raspy and almost broken.

A roar echoed through her mind.

The vexsnare. That was the creature that attacked the girl protecting Sophia. And it had a taste for her blood. The monster was vicious and *always* finished its hunt. Sophia knew it was coming and wouldn't stop until it was dead.

Somehow, she knew the duchess was in trouble. The Nameless Master wanted to take her place.

CHAPTER THIRTY-FOUR
EZEKIEL

*E*zekiel swallowed hard. The monster was there with them. The massive creature was beyond anything he could compare it to, and for once, he had no desire to pull out his book and write down notes about the creature. Of course, that would wait until after the fight was over. If he survived.

Meanwhile, Sophia was on the ground, and she had yet to awaken. They had to hold off the creature until she woke. Ezekiel worried that there had been too much weight on her shoulders recently. He knew she barely slept while in the mountain. Even though she didn't seem to need it. He studied the way the mountain magic seemed to affect her in ways that it didn't touch them. That information led him to more discoveries on the mystery that surrounded Sophia and her past, but he would keep his findings to himself until he was sure. He didn't want to give false hope to Sophia. She needed definitive information, and he had a little more research to do before he could tell her much of anything.

Andreas moved to Sophia's side, and Edric stood at Ezekiel's other side. Ezekiel stood to Sophia's left as the tunnel they were in seemed more like a passageway for soldiers to storm the surface than being used for supplies as he had originally thought. He wasn't quite sure where the tunnel would lead them, but he knew for sure the location wouldn't be good. Not with this creature.

Haris groaned behind them, stomping at the ground. He nudged Sophia with his snout, and her eyes fluttered.

"Mmm... tiny morsels," the creature uttered in a dark, gravelly voice. It sniffed the air and said, "My meal has been delivered to me."

Ezekiel forced back a shudder. He felt strength returning to him, being closer to the surface. The pull of the mountain magic was diluted here. They needed to wake up Sophia now. "Keep nudging her, Haris."

The creature zeroed in on them and let out a loud roar.

Sophia startled awake, and she climbed to her feet as she focused on the vexsnare.

Ezekiel studied her. She didn't seem phased that she had passed out in the middle of the tunnel. He wanted to think that she fainted, but it seemed deeper than that. He would have to wait and ask her after everything was done and over with, when they were safe and out of the threatening grasp of the terrifying creature, talking about eating them.

She returned his gaze with a small smile and a nod.

She was fine. He accepted that look for as much and pulled on the energy that pooled underneath his skin. There wasn't much yet, but he felt it returning as the seconds trickled by.

Sophia and Edric both pulled on their swords. The creature charged. As it drew closer, Sophia met with it, looking tiny in comparison to the massive creature. Ezekiel quickly summoned fire and tossed it at the creature, hitting it with blazing flames. When that did nothing but anger it further, he sent ice toward it, hoping it would numb the creature's limbs and make it slower.

As the vexsnare advanced, and Zeke drained his power the more he used it, they were pushed deeper into the tunnel, coming up to a sealed gate with magical wards.

Edric and Andreas lunged at the creature, taking jabs where they could and avoiding the dangerously sharp claws that swung at them. With each successful jab at the creature, the closer to the warded gate they drew.

Once their backs were pressed to it, Ezekiel said, "Let's get him to charge the gate!"

Edric said, "How do you suppose we do that?"

Ezekiel smiled and shifted his gaze to Edric, "Piss him off."

Edric balked, but he jabbed the tip of his sword at the creature while Sophia shot fire at it. Andreas danced in front of it, and Ezekiel shot daggers of ice. Each shot drove the vexsnare a step backward. It would shake its head and growl with each attack. The plan was working.

Finally, when the creature had enough, it lowered his horned head and snorted, running its back legs behind him to gain more traction.

"When he charges, press against the wall!" Edric shouted.

Everyone braced for the charge. And when the creature did, they dodged to the opposite sides and pressed against the wall as the creature rammed the gate. It shuddered but didn't give way.

"Let's do it again!" Sophia called out and started attacking the creature, shifting between the point of her sword and blasting fire at it.

They repeated the maneuver two more times before the creature broke through. Instantly, screams of fear and terror filled the air, echoing back to them.

"Shit, this led right into Nighthelm!" Edric said,

rushing after the creature. Sophia, Andreas, and Ezekiel rushed after him.

The tunnel led out from underneath the castle and right into the town square. The people of Nighthelm fled in terror as the creature became distracted by all the fleeing food.

They quickly surrounded the vexsnare, repeating the same tactic over and over again. The vexsnare snapped its sharp teeth at them and swiped at them with its razor-like claws. It managed to get Ezekiel in the arm. Stinging, burning pain rocked through him, blurring his vision and making his casting more difficult.

Still, he didn't miss a beat and launched more ice at him. This time in its face. The creature roared and clawed at its muzzle to attempt to free the ice from its vision.

"Prey blinded me," it said. "Prey die worse now."

Sophia let out a loud battle cry, and her whole body was covered in the electric arcs. A purplish-blue aura surrounded her, and she lifted from the ground. Her eyes turned white, and she crossed her body with her arms.

"Take cover!" Ezekiel yelled, and he, Andreas, and Edric dashed behind carts and into alleyways behind barrels.

CHAPTER THIRTY-FIVE
SOPHIA

Sophia knew exactly what this creature was. It was the thing that had broken her soul. Her past hovered at the forefront of her mind as everything she went through, the person she was, was all part of this creature and what it had done to her. It was the weapon, sure, but that didn't ease the ache for revenge that burned in her gut, twisting and knotting her insides as the magic threatened to overtake her again.

She worried she would turn into that once helpless little girl again. The one that couldn't fight for herself, let alone know how. The feeling started to overwhelm her, and she shifted her gaze to her men. They stood by her side, fighting even though they were injured and weakened by the mountain magic. Her worry shifted into resolve.

Rather than running from her past or suppressing it further, she continued to replay those memories. And the more she replayed them, the more her magic wanted to burst from her. But she remained in control. She wasn't that little girl, frightened and hunted. She was stronger than that.

The creature leapt to the side, trying to swipe at a little girl hiding between the carts. Sophia rushed to the vexsnare and thumped it on its head, shoving the tip of her sword into the shoulder belonging to the arm that reached for the girl. The mother rushed to the crying child and held her close as she darted back away from the fighting.

"You took my snack," the creature said and swiped at the carts. It tried to climb the wall to get away, but Ezekiel shot a bolt of lightning at the creature, making it fall back to the ground. Its body weight reduced the carts and tables used for selling goods to mere splinters and firewood.

The damage to the town center was getting out of hand. Sophia needed to do something to get this creature to stop. It seemed nearly indestructible, and though everything she had learned about the creatures saying they were hard to kill, that didn't make it impossible.

But she and her men needed so much more than just the sword and Ezekiel's magic to take this creature out. She needed to do something she hoped she would never have to do again... let her uncontrollable magic free.

She searched around her and quickly realized how impossible it would be for her to let her magic out without killing too many innocents. She didn't want to lose even just one. She had managed to gain control over herself and her magic to take out that creature they had first bumped into in the mountain. She almost lost herself then. She couldn't risk almost losing herself now.

There had to be a way. And with her magic boiling dangerously close to the surface and pushing her to the edge of her control, she didn't know what else to do.

The creature snapped at another citizen and swiped its claw at yet another.

That's it.

She screamed as loud as she could and pulled everything she could within her center. Tingling sensations prickled her skin all along her body. She vaguely heard Ezekiel shout something about taking cover. She held her magic in as long as she could. Then, she released it.

Instead of blacking out and waking up naked, with everything around her incinerated and reduced to ashes, the buildings shook, and the ground cracked open. The beast in front of her took the brunt of the magic, becoming consumed in white light.

Once the light faded, her vision returned to normal. Sophia stared at the remains in the middle of the road, where a large, charred lump of bone and horn lay in place of the vexsnare.

The men left their cover and joined her, each of them taking in the sight of what was left of the vexsnare, and each looked at Sophia with an expression of shock and awe. She met their gazes, panting to catch her breath. Their eyes roamed the entire length of her body, searching for injuries. But Sophia stood unscathed.

Ezekiel shook his head as a grin pulled on his lips. "Sophia, you never cease to amaze me."

Sophia smiled. She felt powerful, and more importantly, in control.

Andreas floated closer and shifted back to his human form. Haris emerged from the tunnel and quickly leaned into him, helping to hold him up.

Sophia gasped at the sight of his blood-soaked clothes. Haris's form glowed and encompassed Andreas. She stared in awe as she watched Haris lend some of his magic to Andreas. It helped to heal him enough so he could stand on his own, but not enough to stave off the injury.

Ezekiel and Edric lent a hand to Andreas, each wrapping an arm around him to help steady him.

Sophia watched citizens coming out from around the corners and quickly uttered the word to have Haris return to her forearm. Haris dissolved into bright, glowing, green mist and floated to her arm, returning as the vibrant reflection of himself. She patted the spot with a smile and whispered a word of thanks for his help. She would have to release him later, when they were alone, to thank him in person. For now, she was comforted that he was safe and out of sight from people who enjoyed the idea of kill first and ask questions later.

Exhaustion started to run its course through her as she approached the monster and knelt before it.

More citizens appeared, and they stood around, gawking at the creature, Sophia, and her men. She slowly stood, hoping there wouldn't be another fight. Afterall, she was exposed as an *anima contritum*—a thing that shouldn't exist—and her men were convicted as being her accomplices.

A fight, she could expect and deal with. But what happened next shocked her most of all.

One by one, the citizens of Nighthelm gathered around her, cheering and applauding her and her men. They all approached and kicked the beast, then shook her hand. She looked to her men as they beamed, shaking hands with the citizens as well.

The people lifted them into the air, bouncing them up and down.

Sophia had never expected fame or recognition for protecting the people of the only home she ever really knew. But having their acceptance and praise—their thanks—she found the sensation to her liking. She enjoyed it, for she knew that it wouldn't last forever.

CHAPTER THIRTY-SIX

SOPHIA

The celebration came to a swift end as all of Nighthelm's army filled the streets. Archers stood on building tops and at the tallest windows with arrows pointed directly at them. The citizens slowly set Sophia and her men down and backed away, fear contorting their faces.

So much for the praise and acceptance.

Even the wraith army filtered into the streets. She turned toward Andreas, and the frown that pulled at his lips said it all. He wasn't expecting them to side with Nighthelm. To stand against him.

Her and her men formed a circle with their backs toward each other. She knew they were drained, but they still prepared to fight. Ezekiel seemed far improved from the skeletal appearance he had from before. It seemed the longer he was topside, the better he felt. Even Edric had more color in his cheeks and the dark circles under his eyes were nearly gone.

Sophia, however, felt just as strong and in control as she did in the mountain. She suspected that she would feel weaker outside of the range of the magic, but she didn't. It was like all of her magic stayed with her.

Booing echoed through the crowd as the soldiers made every effort to push the people back and surround Sophia and her team. Her eyes darted over the number of faces and was surprised to find that the people were defending her and her men.

Some of the people started to push back and the soldiers used rough shoves to force them away from her and her men.

A shuffle happened behind Sophia. She twisted slightly to look over her shoulder as Andreas's people shifted to their wraith forms and protectively surrounded Sophia, Edric, Ezekiel and Andreas. She felt a burst of pride and joy at the sight of the guards' faces. She forced herself not to giggle, but the men looked completely terrified.

She didn't blame them. Several dozen wraith soldiers daring to stand against the soldiers of Nighthelm. The wraiths had always been feared. They were misunderstood, outcasted, shunned because they were different than normal humans. Served them right, just about now. The only people that didn't cower away were the citizens, albeit standing by a bit more cautiously.

Andreas said, "They stand for you, Sophia."

A pinch formed in the middle of her forehead. "Why?"

"They support your magic," he said.

"Well, I for one," Edric said, "am happy to see them."

Ezekiel said, "I as well. Though, it looked a bit questionable for a moment there."

"I agree," Andreas said. "But we are loyal to a fault. Even when appearances suggest otherwise."

The soldiers attacked. The wraiths took on the first ones to step forward. Edric and Ezekiel separated from Andreas and Sophia. While the other two were handling themselves rather well in the fight, Andreas was not.

Sophia worried for him. He could barely stand, and that injury he sustained in the mountain really took a sizable chunk of his strength with it. She couldn't leave him to fight alone, even with his wraith brethren.

She helped him take on two of the three men that filtered through the wall of wraiths.

Three against one didn't seem like a fair fight, even though on his better days, Andreas would make that look too easy. Three against two? Now that was some better odds. Sophia took on the first, quickly deflecting the swing of his sword and shoving hers into his gut. She then turned and jabbed with her blade again, but he saw it coming. He parried and lunged, narrowly missing Sophia's arm. She sidestepped and kicked him in his gut then ran her blade across his throat. When she turned, Andreas had taken out his soldier and readied for the next.

There was a part in the cluster of wraiths and soldiers, revealing Winston as he ran away.

"Winston, that coward," Sophia said. "He's running away again."

"Go after him. I'll be okay. My brothers will help me."

She faced him, worry filling her. "Are you sure?"

He smiled and nodded just as another soldier came. Andreas winced as he took out the soldier, and a wraith joined his side. "Yeah," he said. "Kick his ass."

She kissed him on the cheek and said, "Don't die." Before he could say anything, she darted into the crowd, heading in the direction she saw Winston go.

Something told her, despite everything that had already happened. Her long day of fighting was just beginning.

CHAPTER THIRTY-SEVEN
EZEKIEL

At some point, Ezekiel was separated from Edric. He managed to keep himself free of any injuries, but he was starting to wear down. His movements slowed, and his energy was drained. After taking out a group of soldiers, Tryce Klatrix approached him.

Ezekiel took in a slow, deep breath. Of all the times to face the top sorcerer of his time, this wasn't it.

Tryce nodded once. Ezekiel did the same.

"I've heard a great deal about you, young one," Tryce said. His voice came out strong despite his age. Ezekiel realized he hadn't really heard the man speak before.

"Your reputation precedes you as well," Ezekiel said.

Tryce nodded. "Indeed."

The man went to turn and walk away, or so Ezekiel thought. But he spun around and threw a gale of wind toward him. Ezekiel quickly crossed his arms in front of him, slid his palms down the length of his arms, and ended with his hands crossed, fingers splayed out wide to block the wind. His feet slid along the ground and he let out a grunt as the force hit him.

So that's how you want to play it...

Ezekiel summoned a ball of bright white light and threw it at the sorcerer, who easily dissolved the blinding spell with a wave of his hand.

"Not bad," Tryce said. "I believe you can do better. Come on, boy."

Ezekiel didn't want to know what the man thought he was doing. The last thing he needed was to be exhausted from the fight and end up bed-ridden for days on end. It was bad enough he felt that was the direction he headed in to begin with. But to face off with a man like Tryce? That was insanity. However, it didn't seem like he had much of a choice in the matter. Ezekiel stared dumbfounded at the sorcerer.

Tryce shook his head and threw a bolt of lightning at Ezekiel's feet. "Fight me."

Ezekiel shook his head. A fight with the great sorcerer, Tryce Klatix, would end in death for sure. Despite being the top sorcerer of Nighthelm, Ezekiel's skills weren't quite as powerful as the old man's. As it were, it was frowned upon for any sorcerer to reject a challenge. Even if that challenge would result in certain death.

Ezekiel sighed. *Very well. If it is a fight he wants, then it will be a fight he gets.* He planted his feet shoulder-width apart and narrowed his eyes on the sorcerer. The man was quite a few years older than him. Legendary in his skill and in manipulation of magical energy. Defeating him would not be easy. In fact, it would be impossible. It would take years—decades, even—to even begin to touch the level that Tryce stood at in terms of skill and power. Ezekiel would have to outwit the man and pray that he didn't die in the process.

He started uttering words, moving his hands and fingers in the arcane ways, pulling the energy from around him into his solar plexus. His body started to glow with blue, pulsing energy.

Tryce prepared himself, pulling energy into his own body, moving expertly. Each rotation of a wrist or downward stroke of an arm was careful and smooth. His lips moved with his own incantations. Ezekiel knew the man saw what he was doing and that led him to switch up his tactic.

He threw a ball of fire at the man's feet. Tryce dismissed it without so much as missing a beat in his chant.

Damn it. He saw that coming.

Tryce flicked his wrist and the ground shook

beneath Ezekiel's feet. His chanting faltered, causing him to quickly refocus to regain his momentum.

Once he had pulled enough energy into him, Ezekiel let the energy pulse from his hands straight toward the old man. Ezekiel uttered, *"Infernicus,"* and the beam turned to fire.

Tryce shot out a powerful force of his own, meeting Ezekiel's about halfway between them. Steam rose from the center.

Ezekiel realized that the sorcerer met his spell with ice.

Switching it up, he uttered *"Fulgur."* His fire was replaced with purple lightning, cutting through Tryce's ice like nothing.

The sorcerer's lips pressed into a thin line as his ice quickly changed to bluish-white lightning, causing a loud crack and burst of air where the two currents met. Men from around them staggered and fell to their knees.

Ezekiel took a hard step forward in an effort to close the gap between the two. Tryce met his movements. His arms shook from the pulse of energy, the force of the resistance, and he questioned just how smart it was to make that move. But there was no turning back now. He had to finish this. He had to try to survive this.

Step-by-step, the gap closed until they were just a few paces from each other. Sparks and light and electrical arcs flew around them, reaching out to the soldiers that stopped fighting to watch the dual between sorcerers. Ezekiel maintained his spell with great difficulty. His arms started to shake from the strain of his spell against his opponent. Sweat trickled down the side of his head, soaking the collar of his shirt while it seemed Tryce had yet to even have so much as a bead of wetness along his.

Ezekiel closed his eyes against the end he knew was coming any second. There was a shudder in the magic between them. His eyes opened.

Red dots dribbled down the sorcerer's forehead. Ezekiel almost lost focus with the realization that Tryce struggled in their magical duel—against *him*. It would be easy to defeat the man in that moment, to send a spell flying toward him and quickly cutting him down. But something within Ezekiel wouldn't allow him to. The look in Tryce's eyes told him that he knew the same thing and just waited for him to end it and take the place of the greatest sorcerer alive.

No.

He stepped to the side, releasing the pulse of energy between them, creating a loud thunderclap. Tryce fell to his knees. Ezekiel approached the man and held out a hand to help him up. Tryce nodded once. Ezekiel did the same. Tryce faced him as he worked to catch his breath.

"You have done well," he said. "Not many people

could hold up for as long as you have or so easily withstand me as an opponent."

Ezekiel stared at the man like he started speaking a different language. "Thank you?" He didn't mean for it to come out like a question. But it had.

Tryce held out his hand and said, "No. Thank you, boy. You fought with honor, and where I come from, it's something we hold in high regard. You showed me respect, and you stood your ground. You are not what Winston would have us all believe—and might I add, as a sorcerer, you are an equal."

Ezekiel slowly took the man's hand. He gave it a firm shake. "It's an honor, sir."

He smiled, released Ezekiel's hand and walked off. Just like that. Nothing else said or done. Ezekiel continued to stare after the sorcerer long after he disappeared. He still wasn't sure what had happened or just quite how to process everything. The last thing he thought he would ever earn was the respect of a man so revered and feared as Tryce Klatrix.

CHAPTER THIRTY-EIGHT
EDRIC

*E*dric lost track of who was friend or foe. So many of the men he served with now fought him. And so many of those men he used to consider friends. It pained him that they were blinded by greed and led to believe the lies that Winston had spread. Their deaths were ultimately meaningless. Their honor stripped because they followed a corrupt leader.

He couldn't blame them. Had it been him in their shoes, he probably would've done the same. He was such a devoted solider, believing in serving justice and protecting the city—his city—above all else.

But that was before he met Sophia. She changed him. She changed everything.

More men whom he had served with stood toe-to-

toe with him. And he cut them down. It was him or them.

Eventually, he pushed his feelings down. He hated the guilt that came with fighting his old comrades. That feeling only increased with each man he knew, practically raised with, and watched the light from their eyes fade away. He had no choice but to move automatically, shutting down feelings and going into full survival mode.

That was until Marlow.

Edric spun around, pulling his sword from another fallen ally to lock blades with him. Marlow's eyes widened in recognition, and a smile crossed the man's face.

"I always knew you would fall off your pedestal someday, *Commander*."

Edric shrugged off the way he emphasized commander and said, "And I always knew you would be the first in line to try and replace me."

The man chuckled low and dark. "Oh, I didn't try. I *did*. And you will now taste my blade with the other traitors that refused to abandon loyalty to you."

Edric pushed him off his sword and the man stepped back completely at ease, as though he saw the opportunity to fight him as nothing more than a regular sparring match. But this wasn't practice. And Marlow knew better than to underestimate Edric's ability to strategize and exploit weaknesses of his opponents.

Marlow held his sword at the ready, same ridiculous grin on his face. "Just like old times, eh?"

Edric shook his head. "You have no idea what you are getting yourself into."

Marlow shrugged. "Sure, I do. I kill you, and then the duchess will promote me to commander."

"You may try to kill me, but I assure you, Marlow, I. Will. Not. Fall." Edric lunged.

Marlow parried Edric's sword thrust with an attack of his own, landing the blade nearly in the center of Edric's forearm. Had he not moved at the right time, he would have lost an arm.

Edric glared at the man who just smiled in return.

"I've been practicing," Marlow said, prideful grin and all. "Can't you tell?"

Edric didn't answer, instead he followed Marlow's steps, carefully watching for each twitch and movement. Marlow never sucked at being a swordsman. Quite the contrary. But when it came to skill versus skill, Edric always stood heads above the rest. He was bred for things like this. Marlow was born with a silver spoon in his mouth and enough money to buy his way into the academy and avoiding the dirty jobs that the rest of the new recruits had to do. His money also bought him the best trainers and tutors.

He almost came close to earning Edric's respect

during a sparring match. The way he held himself was almost like that of a seasoned soldier. It impressed Edric to see the skill. But then he saw through the man. Trying to buy his way through the ranks.

Bile rose in his throat as he lunged for another attack. He missed Marlow. But just barely. He shook his head. "Doesn't seem like all those training sessions did you any good. You can hold a sword. And your stance is correct. But you lack an inherent concept all soldiers have."

Marlow parried the next attack and said, "And what would that be, great, fallen commander?"

Edric moved, crossing his sword over Marlow's and flicking his wrist. Marlow's sword landed feet from him. His eyes widened in fear. Edric forced down the satisfaction of seeing the apprehension in his eyes as it would never do to let his guard down, even for a show of pride.

As Marlow scrambled to reclaim his blade, Edric said, "Lack of fear for getting hurt."

Edric attacked, his thrusts, lunges, downward strokes, and slashes came too quick. Marlow struggled to block each hit of the blade but received cuts he had never had the pleasure of experiencing before. With each strike Edric stepped forward, pushing Marlow up against the wall, leaving the coward without an exit.

Marlow's eyes were wild with fright and his

breaths quickened as he desperately searched for a way out of the fight.

Edric shook his head. "You will never command an army. You will never make the sacrifices it takes to lead men to their deaths. You are, and always will be, nothing but a spoiled brat. Your money will never buy loyalty."

Marlow's gasps came with little squeaks, and though Edric didn't look, he was sure the man wet himself just then.

"You wouldn't dare kill me," he said. "It would only look worse on you."

"Care to take a wager on that?" he asked as he pointed the tip of his blade at Marlow's heart, or where it should've been. To add his point further, he put a little pressure, enough to puncture the nice, expensive leather vest he wore.

Marlow tried to press himself even farther into the wall. As he lifted his hands, he released his sword, sending it clanking to the ground.

Edric cocked his head to the side and narrowed his gaze on his old comrade. "Call off the men."

Marlow's mouth moved but he didn't form words.

A little more pressure into the tip of his sword and Edric said, "Call off your men. Now."

"Retreat," Marlow's voice squeaked.

Edric shook his head. "You'll have to do better than that."

"Retreat!" Marlow's voice came out stronger. "Fall back!"

Edric took a step back from him, removing the sword from Marlow's chest. "I suggest you figure out just where your loyalties lie before they get you killed."

Marlow nodded quickly and rushed away, leaving behind his sword and a puddle from where he had stood. Edric shook his head again as he reached over and picked up the sword. He sheathed both of them into his belt around his waist then went to find Andreas, Ezekiel, and Sophia.

Something about that whole interaction told him the fall back was just a temporary thing. He wanted to make sure the use of the time they were just given was enough to get them the hell out of there before they showed up with reinforcements.

CHAPTER THIRTY-NINE

SOPHIA

Sophia cornered Winston in the old market place. He turned and smiled at her. Bile rose in the back of her throat and she realized he purposefully led her here. He shook his head and ran his fingers through his hair, then held his arms out to the side.

"Sophia, oh, Sophia. You are so predictable."

She rolled her eyes and crossed her arms. "How so?"

"I knew you would follow me here. You did exactly what I wanted you to. You see? I knew you wanted me."

"What I want," Sophia said, "is my sword and dagger back. Your head on a pike would be a nice addition."

He chuckled, shaking his head. "This cat and

mouse game has grown tiring. This cat wants his reward. Give in to me, Sophia. Make it easier on yourself. I would hate to hurt a hair on that pretty head of yours by forcing you."

She cocked an eyebrow at that. "You? Hurt me?" She scoffed. "You really are delusional."

"I was hoping you would say that. Makes a firm hand a bit more meaningful." Winston held out the sword and dagger with each hand. "These really are some peculiar weapons. A proper woman wouldn't have need for them, would she?"

Sophia narrowed her gaze on him, wishing he would hurry up and get to the point. She hated all this monologue. He really loved hearing himself talk. Too bad for him, she didn't share in that. "They are mine, regardless. Return them to me or I will pry them from your dead, cold fingers."

He smiled wickedly and said, "Challenge accepted."

An amulet around his neck glowed with dim blue light. His eyes took on the color and he used the sword to attack Sophia with a lot more force than he naturally had. She wasn't expecting the force at first and stumbled a little, but she quickly recovered and returned the attack. He smacked her and it was like lightning shooting through her skull.

She held her cheek for a moment and pursed her brows. He didn't have magic or abilities to wield it. He was just a stupid, puny, asshole of a human. Recovering, she stood a bit taller and rolled out her shoulders before stretching her neck from side to side.

Two can play this game.

She shot electrical sparks toward him. He dodged and the hit slammed into the corner of a building.

He looked at the damage, shook his head, and made a tsking sound with his tongue. "Now, now, Sophia. Careful of the damage you do. You wouldn't want the people to believe in that pesky little accusation of yours, hmm?" He paced in front of her.

He was right. Unfortunately. Part of the rumor was that she wanted to destroy Nighthelm. If she was going to maintain the progress she made with the people, she would have to keep the collateral damage to a minimum if she could help it. Though it didn't help that Winston managed to cheat and get his hands on magical artifacts that gave him powers he didn't know how to handle much less should have in the first place. Magic was a fickle thing, and someone as power hungry as Winston should never have been allowed such access. Even now, the power corrupted him, poisoning his blood like the mountain magic would. His skin held a sickly glow and perspiration soaked his shirt. His body slightly trembled. It was as if he had extreme difficulty holding on to the power the amulets gave him. The man was completely out of his league. Sophia shook her head.

"Where did you get the amulet?" she asked as she

matched his pacing, keeping a safe distance from his blade and the magic he had no idea how to use.

He shrugged. "I have my resources."

She remembered him telling her that he had ways of bringing her back from the dead. Making her his, whether she wanted him or not. A sharp twist in her gut made her bite the inside of her cheek. The bile rose in her throat and she had to take a few deep breaths to keep the nausea at bay. The last thing she wanted was to empty her stomach in front of him and give him the time to slap on whatever he had that he thought would make her obedient.

"You don't know what you are doing," she said and thrust with her sword. He parried, attacked with his own, and she quickly blocked the attack, kicking him in the stomach.

"I have more control over this than you could ever hope to have over your magic."

She smiled. "You have no idea."

She tossed a ball of fire at him. He caught it and threw it back. It grew bigger as it rushed toward her, and she had to duck and roll out of the way to avoid getting hit with it. He laughed. She turned her attention to him and glared. The magic pulsed deep within her, steadily rising to the surface. She didn't want to have an episode in the middle of Nighthelm, despite the control she had gained over her magic. But if it meant taking out this nightmare of a man, she would gladly do so, and deal with the repercussions of the actions with a smile on her face.

He shot purple lightning at her and she worked hard to dodge the bolts as she pulled out the same tactic and thought of how she could conjure ice. Or, perhaps, anything that would get him to just fucking die already.

He continued to laugh as he threw magic after magic at her, and she tried to do the same. It was all a game to him. And he had no idea the control of the power she had.

Having had enough of this, she charged him, sword at the ready, and knocked him to the ground. She straddled him, with her knees on his shoulders, and pounded at his face with her fists. Little zaps of energy sparked along her knuckles and left the man's skin charged in spots. She pulled at the amulet and tossed it behind her and cut off the hands that had rings, and even pulled off a wrist cuff that she assumed enhanced his newfound abilities. Anything she suspected of helping him, she got rid of. She ignored his screams and the loud cries for help.

Standing, she took back her sword and dagger and then stared down at him. Holding out her hand over his body, she closed her eyes as a small, white ball of concentrated, wild magic burst from her hand and incinerated the bastard.

Standing back, she watched as he turned to ashes.

Her gaze then shifted to the sword. It glowed at her touch. It was the first time she held it without her gloves. Reminded of what happened with the oracles, she quickly sheathed her sword and dagger. The sword was such a powerful artifact. She didn't want to accidently destroy it and fail in her purpose to restore the crown.

She stayed for a few moments longer as she absorbed the heavy moment of when Grindel gave her the dagger and how he had died because of Winston and the Nameless Master. After letting a few tears fall, she wiped them away and went to find and rejoin her men. She hoped Andreas fared well. Though she trusted his wraith brethren, she worried about him fighting in the condition she left him in. That thought urged her feet forward and her pace quicker. The sooner she got back to her men, the better.

CHAPTER FORTY

SOPHIA

Halfway back to the town's center, alarms rocked throughout Nighthelm. The people had returned to their homes and likely locked all their doors and windows. Marching feet started echoing through the streets, and Sophia knew they would never survive another fight. Especially with Nighthelm's entire army.

She found her men with the wraiths in the town center. She breathed a relieved sigh as she wrapped her arms around each of her men and placed a kiss on their cheeks. She was glad they were relatively unharmed. Andreas even seemed to have been doing better. He smiled at her.

Edric said, "We have to go. The soldiers will be here any moment now."

Sophia nodded. "Where can we go?"

"I talked with my brothers," Andreas said. "We have a town we set up in case of persecution. We have been invited to join them."

"We can't stay here any longer," Ozul said. "Not now that we openly stood against Nighthelm guard."

Sophia frowned. She didn't think of the consequences at the time. Now she felt responsible for alienating an entire race from their homes. "I'm sorry."

Mica snorted. "Don't be. We're liberated." He smiled, and she felt a little better. Not much, but still. "We have to go now."

"Lead the way," Sophia said.

Her and her men followed the wraiths through the Shade to an exit at the far end of the city. They filtered through the gate and fled into the woods. Sophia kept her eyes peeled for grimms. They were still after her. Thankfully, the alarms from Nighthelm faded into the distance. Not long after that, the group's pace slowed to an even march.

The trees grew thinner, and Sophia could see the tiny houses and a firepit already lit. Other wraiths were already there, setting up shops and settling in. Once she crossed the threshold, she let out a breath she hadn't realized she had been holding. The tension in her shoulders eased, and Andreas led them to a small house nearby that was reserved for them.

After settling down for the evening, they were able to enjoy a hot meal and fill their bellies. Sophia relaxed with her men. Andreas was all bandaged up and looking better than ever. She smiled as she was grateful his injuries weren't worse. It was too close this time, and she would never be able to live with herself if the worst had happened.

But it didn't. And she thanked her lucky stars for that.

"What do we do now?" Ezekiel said. "Nighthelm is sort of off limits and we still have yet to figure out who that girl is."

Sophia nodded. "First, I think a good night's rest will do us all some good."

"I agree," Edric said. "But we do need to come up with a plan."

"Sleep first," Andreas said. "We can talk about plans and taking over the world tomorrow."

"Hopefully, the Nameless Master won't usurp the duchess before then," Sophia said. But she knew he was right. They had fought long and hard. They needed the time to rest and recuperate without further talk of war on the horizon.

"How do you know that?" Ezekiel asked.

Sophia shrugged. "I just do. It happened right before the vexsnare attacked. I can't explain it, but it was like I knew these things."

Ezekiel stared at her, waiting for more information. When she didn't speak, he added, "That's it? Nothing else?"

"For now, that is it. I'll talk about the rest later." Sophia laid back on the ground, tucking her arms behind her head. The stars above them twinkled brightly, and a gentle breeze blew over her, giving her a small reprieve from the heat of the fire nearby. She smiled to herself as her men laid down next to her.

Sophia had come so far from where she was just a short time ago. She was so close to living up to the purpose the oracles had given her. Though she still had a long road ahead of her, she felt closer than ever to the heirs. She felt it deep within her, filling her with hope.

Rest now. Fight later.

Before she realized it, her eyes had become difficult to keep open. She was safe where she was, with her men and the wraiths. All she had to do was sleep. Peaceful, restful, and well-earned. And with that, her eyes closed, and she drifted off.

YOU'RE MISSING OUT…

Olivia Ash occasionally takes over the Wispvine Publishing social media channels on Facebook, Instagram, and Twitter.

Olivia also likes to hang out with Lila Jean in their Facebook group specifically for readers like you to come together and share their lives and interests, especially regarding the hot guys from their reverse harem novels. Please check it out and join in whenever you get the chance! Everyone in there is amazing, and you'll fit right in.

https://www.facebook.com/groups/LilaJeanOliviaAsh/

Sign up for email alerts of new releases AND exclusive access to bonus content, book recommendations, and more!

https://wispvine.com/newsletter/nighthelm-academy-email-signup/

Enjoying the series? Awesome! Help others discover The Nighthelm Guardian Series by leaving a review at Amazon.

http://mybook.to/Nighthelm1

ABOUT THE AUTHOR

OLIVIA ASH

Olivia Ash spends her time dreaming up the perfect men to challenge, love, and protect her strong heroines (who actually don't need protecting at all). Her stories are meant to take you on a journey into the world of the characters and make you want to stay there.

Reviews are the best way to show Olivia that you care about her stories and want other people discover them. If you enjoyed this novel, please consider leaving a review at Amazon. Every review helps the author and she appreciates the time you take to write them.

ABOUT THE AUTHOR

Dede Hall

Dede Ash spends her days dreaming up new men to challenge love, and prides her stories on their (wholesomely) don't-need-protecting attitude. Her stories are meant to be more than just escapades into the world of the darkly romantic but a view into our own time.

She writes to her own rules, knows that you care about her characters and wants you to care about them. If you adore romance novels, please consider leaving a review. A novel is every reader's link to the author, and she appreciates the time you took to write them.

Printed in the USA
CPSIA information can be obtained
at www.ICGtesting.com
LVHW040005030924
789950LV00031B/781